COVENTRY LIBRARIES
WITHDRAWN
FOR SALE

Trailing Wing

With the tough cattle drive from Colorado to Wyoming finally over, Jubal Lorde looked forward to buying some land and settling down in the peaceful town of Pitchfork . . . until someone stole his herd and killed his friend Billy. Suddenly, Jubal had a new reason for staying in town.

Now he must pit himself against the tough, influential businessman Kingsley Post and his mercenary henchman, Grif Bartow . . . but will the desire for revenge prove worthwhile when it comes to the final showdown?

By the same author

Ironhead
The Landbreakers
The Frightened Valley
Borderline
Death Song
Shot Gold
Punchers Creek
Hog-Tied
Freighter's Way
Brevet Ridge
The Bull Chop
Wolf Hole
Rio Bonito

Trailing Wing

Abe Dancer

ROBERT HALE · LONDON

© Abe Dancer 2010
First published in Great Britain 2010

ISBN 978-0-7090-8934-6

Robert Hale Limited
Clerkenwell House
Clerkenwell Green
London EC1R 0HT

www.halebooks.com

The right of Abe Dancer to be identified as
author of this work has been asserted by him
in accordance with the Copyright, Designs and
Patents Act 1988

COVENTRY CITY LIBRARIES	
3 8002 01894 971 1	
HJ	26-Jul-2010
	£13.25
CEN	

Typeset by
Derek Doyle & Associates, Shaw Heath
Printed and bound in Great Britain by
CPI Antony Rowe, Chippenham and Eastbourne

1

They reached Owl Creek by late afternoon, and tomorrow they would push the herd into the valley. It would end the long drive that had brought them halfway across Colorado to Pitchfork, Wyoming. Jubal Lorde had been riding swing, but now the herd were bedded down on grassland that climbed towards the Wind River timberline. He was a tall, loose-limbed man, his features dark, weather-beaten after weeks on the trail. His canvas jacket was scarred with use. His jeans were faded and threadbare, and the brim of his hat had gained the wilt of age.

A spring drizzle was falling and Dummy Parsons had parked his chuck wagon under the spreading branches of a live oak. He was stooped over the fire, turning sizzling strips of fat bacon in a pan, when Jubal climbed damp and weary from the saddle. The crew that weren't riding herd were eating under a tarpaulin they had stretched across sapling rails. Billy Box was squinting at a shard of mirror glass that hung against the oak. He was aaaghing, then cussing, then aaaghing again as he shaved in the fading light.

The rain became a hiss on the tarpaulin, but it was warm and comfortable enough by the fire. Jubal sniffed in the smell of the bacon, the beans and coffee, the sharp tang of woodsmoke.

Bull McRae the trail boss, put down his tin plate and winked at Jubal. 'The way he's hackin' himself, he's goin' to run dry,' he drawled, indicating Billy with a nod of his head. 'Chickamauga, was the last time I saw that much blood.'

Billy was twenty-five years old, heavily built and had long blond hair. 'I reckon Dummy's been usin' this razor to cut jerky,' he said with a broad grin.

'For your sake, I hope the girl's worth it,' Parsons said good naturedly. 'Two months of Iris this an' Iris that. You'd think she was one o' them three graces. Here, eat this an' put some lard on your pizzle,' Parsons laughed, and handed Billy a filled plate.

Billy shook his head. 'No more trail slum for me. Startin' tonight, I'm takin' pie off a plate,' he answered, reaching for a scrap of towel to rub his cheeks. 'It's a good feelin' bein' home at last. Hey, Jube,' he called out to Lorde. 'You should've moved out here when me an' Hester did. Wait till you see. The country's so pretty, you want to whistle at it.'

Jubal grinned and took up the plate Parsons had filled. He found a dry spot, sat cross-legged to eat his food customarily quick. But this time it was with more satisfaction and, after he had built a smoke, he watched Billy turn out his traps for a clean shirt.

'You just watch out for that Ase Linder feller. See he don't come after you with a fowlin' piece.' he said. 'You said yourself, he don't take to cowboys sparkin' off his daughters.'

'Yeah, but that was *then*. *Now* I got a third o' this herd bought an' paid for; I'm as good as him or any other man hereabouts,' Billy responded confidently. 'He's goin' to have to get used to seein' me around.'

'Well, all I'm sayin' is, watch your back trail. Didn't someone take a shot at you here last spring?' Jubal recalled.

'Yeah, but a couple o' Linder's riders did too. An' I know *they* weren't takin' a gather on his daughters,' Billy answered with reason. He buckled on his gunbelt and beamed pleasure. 'He said he thought it was me, but he must've known it weren't. Anyway, I ain't lookin' for trouble, Jube. So, are you comin' with me or what? Maybe Iris'll bring her sister to town.'

'I'll have to shave, an' you just put me off that idea,' Jubal answered back. 'But I guess you'll be needin' somebody to watch out for you.'

'Have a scrub instead. Go on, it won't take you but a minute. I'll go saddle us a couple o' fresh horses.' With that, Billy untied Jubal's horse, swung up and rode toward the remuda.

'You think there's goin' to be trouble, Jube?' McRae asked.

Jubal got up and shrugged his shoulders. 'You heard him say he ain't lookin' for any.'

McRae speculated for a moment. 'That ain't exactly what I meant,' he said.

Jubal stripped down, hard muscle gleaming across his shoulders and arms as he stepped into the drizzle. As he cleaned himself with a large block of yellow soap, restless thoughts began to race through his mind. Since meeting up with Billy in Colorado last fall, he'd thought about what it would be like to make a home for himself. Billy obviously had the idea of settling down, getting married and raising a family, and that was just fine, but the thought of him doing the same made him nervous, a bit panicky.

*

Jubal and Billy had fought side by side through four long years of war. They were raw youngsters when they enlisted, twenty-year-old veterans when they returned to what was left of their homes. Jubal's parents had died of fever, and all Billy had left of his family was his sister, Hester. Within days, Billy and Hester had sold the best part of their belongings and joined a wagon train bound for Denver, Colorado. Jubal took the dregs of his wild juices onto long cattle drives. He took work as an army scout in Texas, then deputy marshal in a New Mexico cow town. His restlessness had taken him from Albuquerque in the south to Sheridan in the north. During those rough years, he reckoned his only refuge was in the occasional letters from Billy and Hester.

Jubal had finished shaving and was getting dressed by the time Billy returned with the horses. A few minutes later the pair of them bid farewell and rode from camp.

The steady drizzle continued. Mist hid the tops of the mountains ahead of them, and a cruel grey sky hurried first dark. Snow highlighted the lee of boulders, drifted low against tree trunks where they picked their way down the long slope to the valley road a mile away. Billy rode ahead. Jubal followed a dozen feet behind, the brim of his hat drooping low over his eyes. From time to time he looked up to scan their surroundings, thought it didn't seem much like the Colorado he recalled.

The previous summer, he'd been ramrodding a ranch along the Arkansas River when Billy wrote that he was coming south to buy cattle. In Colorado, cattle were cheap, and Billy had talked two of his neighbours into pooling their money. But hiring competent trail hands who knew the country they'd be driving the herd back through was a problem. Jubal wrote back saying he knew good men, and he'd select the best route for Billy to follow.

Billy duly arrived, but snow fell early that fall. A freezing winter followed, and they decided to start their drive next spring. Meanwhile, they purchased a thousand head of cattle and Billy spoke hopefully of the Wyoming valley. At that time, Jubal didn't even consider going, but what Billy spoke about was more of a certainty than anything else in his life. He started to think about the possibilities, and by the time spring came around, he had made up his mind to go. A bank in Santa Fe held what money he'd got saved, plus what he'd received from the sale of his parents' place. It was enough to buy 500 head of longhorns and to pay his share of the crew's wages. He could lease a strip of grass and set himself up to freight cattle for the Eastern markets.

But now they had the long drive behind them, Jubal felt a curious pinch of captivity, as though his freedom was a life force turning dry. He suddenly missed the anticipation of new places, the risk of new challenges. Perhaps it was foolish to think he would settle down, live with regrets for the rest of his life. He sighed deeply, reminded himself he could still change his mind, that meantime there was cattle to sell.

Billy had followed a trail through a strip of timber and out on to a low bluff. Below, rain pocked the sluggish flow of water through a gully. Beyond it, Jubal saw the road. Its slopes were dark with timber, its ruts full and glazed with run off. The road curved westward, before disappearing in the mist that had settled thickly in the pass.

'We can pick up the road ahead a ways,' Billy called.

They rode to where the bluff fell away. Now, the watercourse churned angrily between gleaming, knuckled boulders, and the road was hidden beneath a torrent of gully water.

Billy cautiously picked his way across the stream and began climbing the short, steep bank.

Jubal was holding his horse, was watching Billy's mount reach its head towards the top of the bank when he heard the sharp crack of the rifle shot. He heard Billy's grunt, saw him sag forward, as he instinctively spurred his own mount up the rise.

Billy started to slip from the saddle, but Jubal had reached him. He dismounted quickly and stretched up a muscular arm. He scanned the road and saw the gunman up ahead. Rain slanted between them, but Jubal could see the man was wearing a blanket coat and a dark, wide-brimmed hat. He was jerking at the reins of a restless mount with one hand while trying to raise his rifle for a second shot. He saw Jubal, and froze for a moment of uncertainty.

Billy groaned with pain and sagged down against Jubal's supporting arm. The horseman fired as Jubal was trying to drag his own rifle from the saddle scabbard, then he wheeled his horse from the road and ran into the trees.

Jubal's gut feeling was to chase, to ride the man down, but Billy gasped again, and he used both arms to lower him carefully to the sodden ground.

The bullet had struck Billy low in the chest. In the fading light, his skin matched the colourless snow. His eyes were closed, he breathed thickly, and Jubal cursed at his friend's suffering.

Billy stiffened, coughed harshly and blood dribbled on to his lips. Then he opened his eyes, dull with the shock of hurt and doubt. 'You ain't goin' to tell me it was Ase Linder an' his ol' fowler, are you?' he croaked out.

'I hardly saw him, Billy. I don't know who he was.'

'I reckon it was someone called Ralph Sand. I didn't have to see him.'

'Who the hell's Ralph Sand?'

'You don't want to know, Jube. Don't get drawn in. An' tell Hester – tell her to sell up,' Billy said quietly. Then he made a smile that was cracked with misery. 'I didn't reckon on goin' like this,' he whispered. 'An' not yet, either.'

Jubal straightened. A roaring fire of anger blotted out all his thoughts other than immediate and brutal revenge. 'Then *don't*,' he rasped. 'I always said you was a mule-headed cuss. Hang on till I come back.'

Jubal spurred his horse along the flooded road. He twisted away where the horseman had disappeared into the trees, but sooty darkness now hung in the increasingly dense timber. He reined in, sat beneath the rain that dripped steadily from the branches above him. There was very little sound, and he dismounted to study the ground for hoof tracks. There was no sign though, and he felt the futility of the chase, kicked at the sodden duff. It looked like the horseman knew his way through the country and, in the gloom, it was impossible for Jubal to track the route any further.

In less than ten minutes he was back, standing deep in thought over Billy. Bitter rage churned inside him, and he ground his jaw at the sight of his friend's hands lifelessly clasping a dark pool of blood. For the first time in many years, he sensed real loneliness, and then the liability hit him. How would he tell Hester about this? He didn't even know Iris Linder, and both girls would be excited and hopeful for Billy's coming home. Jubal cursed violently. Now he had to tell Hester that she'd lost her brother. He recalled the gist of what Billy said she'd told him when he left their home in Colorado. 'If there's any trouble, let that friend o' yours sort it out.'

Jubal soon realized that Billy could have been bushwhacked for something other than cattle business. He didn't know what, but it was stacked that way. As he gazed at the clammy, wraithlike face, he knew that he had to seek out the answer. Beyond what Billy had mentioned, he was a stranger to the territory and knew next to nothing of its problems or its folk. There were a few names, but little else.

'Ralph Sand,' Jubal repeated the name to himself. 'I ain't goin' to get drawn in, Billy boy, but I said I'd look out for you. If it was this man Sand, I *will* shoot him. I promise you *that*,' he growled. He looked around for Billy's horse, but it had wandered away. 'Gone home, probably,' he muttered indifferently. He tied the body across the saddle of his own horse, and, sitting behind the cantle he rode slowly back to the herd.

The rain continued to fall and full dark settled. Jubal smudged the salty wetness across his face. 'Be real wakeful, Mr Sand,' he muttered. 'Not that it'll do you any good.'

2

An hour later, with the hoofs of his horse and those of the pack horse ringing dully, Jubal Lorde picked up the valley road again.

With the help of Bull McRae, he had wrapped Billy in a square of wagon canvas. The crew had watched severe and silent under lamps hung from the chuck wagon. They had liked and respected Billy Box and, bearing the threatening silence in mind, Jubal advised McRae to post guards, see that everyone stayed close in to camp. Right now wasn't the time for a bunch of cowpokes to go tearing the town apart.

The rain had stopped, but mist pressed low as they climbed through the pass. Then the road climbed steeply for a mile before levelling out. One minute vision was no more than twenty or thirty feet, the next Jubal could see stars, clouds floating across a half-moon. Timber fell away on either side, and the road dropped to the grassland beyond. The mountains of Wind River were black silhouettes against the inky sky and, for the first time, Jubal gazed at the vast reach of the valley. He narrowed his eyes at the scattered lights of Pitchfork in the distance, tightened his grip on the lead rope.

The first building at the east end of the main street was a livery stable. Lamplight slanted through its open doors, brought with it the warm, musty odours of the stable. Inside, Jubal could see yellowy mounds of hay and the rumps of horses in their stalls.

A lanky, straggle-haired man in a discoloured coat appeared and stared silently at Jubal. A second man leaned the wooden rake he'd been cleaning the floor with, and moved alongside him.

'I'm lookin' for the sheriff's office,' Jubal said.

'Well this sure ain't it,' the lanky man replied. Then he turned his attention to the pack horse and tugged at the canvas that was wrapped around Billy's body.

'I know. I meant for you to tell me where it was, not get smart,' Jubal snapped back. 'An' keep your hands off my stuff.'

'Your *stuff*, eh?' the man echoed. He ignored the warning and lifted a fold in the canvas.

With both hands, Jubal leaned out and grabbed the man viciously by the hair. At the same time he swung down and out of his saddle, and kicked the man's feet from under him. His face splattered at Jubal's feet, and he spat filthy mud with an obscenity. As fast as he could, he scrambled to his knees and pushed away the flap of his coat.

Jubal gave a small, cold smile in response. 'If there's a gun in there, leave it,' he threatened. 'Dyin' with your maw full o' horse turds ain't the best way to go.'

Very cautiously, the man pushed himself to his feet. Humiliated, he rubbed his muddy palms on the front of his coat. 'You're a mite touchy, feller,' he spluttered, and shuffled out sideways through the livery doors.

'Evenin',' the other man said with a grin as he stepped

forward. 'I'm the hostler. As for Kirkland, well, they don't call him Snoop for nothin'. It'll be the death of him, one day.'

'Or one filthy *night,*' Jubal retorted.

'Is that young Billy Box, you got there?' the hostler continued, his voice tinged with a distinct suggestion of remorse.

'Yeah, that's Billy,' Jubal said. 'You must've knowed him.'

The hostler nodded. 'Not well. I know he was a good man. It's what most others would've known, too,' he replied. 'The sheriff you were askin' about's over in Rockford. That's thirty miles east o' here.'

'What do you do for law meantime?'

'Town marshal. You'll find him in the second buildin' on your right, past the next corner out o' here. Name's Hirkam Jeffs. Him or his deputy should be there. His name's John Tolliver.'

Jubal nodded his thanks, remounted and gave the hostler a hard, penetrating look. 'Anyone else ride into town durin' the last couple of hours?' he asked,

The man cleared his throat 'Might've done. Who's askin'?'

Jubal had a thoughtful moment before saying anything. 'Never mind,' he said, before gently touching spurs to his horse.

There would be a few reasons why the hostler wouldn't tell him if there had been anyone riding in to town, but Jubal didn't and wouldn't know of one. With regard to who'd thought well of Billy, he'd said *most* others. There was some sorrow, but no genuine surprise or question as to what had happened.

Jubal swung down in front of the marshal's office,

looped reins around the hitch rail. Light shone through a long window that was set into the log building. He rested a hand on the canvas-wrapped body, then, mouthing curses, he ducked under the rail and opened the door.

Marshal Jeffs was a spare, sinewy man in his middle years. He was leaning back in his chair, gazing at the ceiling with pale, rheumy eyes. His deputy sat on the corner of the office desk picking at his fingernails. Both of them looked comfortable, at ease with nothing much happening.

The three of them had taken Billy's body to a room out back of the undertaker's. They had returned to the office, where Jubal was now telling his story of the shooting.

'Did you get any sort o' look at him?' Jeffs asked.

'Nothin' that wouldn't fit any goddamn saddle stiff who's wearin' a hat an' coat. I wouldn't exactly recognize him ridin' down the street.'

'An' you say five hundred o' that herd is yours?' John Tolliver wanted to know.

'Yeah, I told you,' Jubal said.

'Another five hundred to Billy Box, an' the rest's for splittin' between Owen Chase an' Dudley Arnwood. Is that right?'

Jubal nodded. 'Yeah, I told you that, too,' he repeated, more brusquely. He knew the questions were necessary, but he had taken a fairly instant dislike to Tolliver, and he didn't like the cynical tone of his voice.

Jubal took a deep breath. He stared at the floor for a moment, then turned to Jeffs. 'But Billy recognized him,' he said with significant timing.

'What? Who?' Tolliver leaned forward, his eyes narrowed. 'Who'd he recognize?'

Jubal hesitated. There was more than legal or neutral

interest in Tolliver's question, but Jubal didn't take his eyes off Jeffs.

'A man called, Sand,' he said.

Almost immediately, Tolliver laughed, nearly clapped his hands. 'Ha, for a moment there, I thought you'd got the key to our case.'

'How'd you mean?' Jubal got in ahead of Jeffs. 'Do you recognize the name?'

'Yeah, an' the feller it comes with. Ralph Sand's been at the KP saloon most o' the afternoon . . . evenin' too. Seen him there myself.'

'Sand ain't possessed o' the most memorable countenance in these parts,' Jeffs said. 'If it was gettin' dark, Billy could have been mistaken. I mean, how sure could he have been?' he offered doubtfully.

'Yeah, there's some say that Sand's so ugly, he must have special powers,' Tolliver went along with Jeffs. 'Well, he sure goddamn has, if he's been playin' monte, down *here* at the same time as bushwhackin' up *there*. If I were *you*, Lorde, I wouldn't go around repeatin' that story.'

'Why not? They weren't my dyin' words. An' besides, you ain't me,' Jubal turned a hostile eye on Tolliver.

The deputy marshal's voice hardened. 'Listen, mister, I used to haul lumber with Ralph, an' I ain't about to have him accused o' murder,' he said.

'No one's accused anyone of anythin' yet,' Jeffs interrupted gruffly. 'Lorde just told you, they was Billy Box's words, not *his*.'

'Who does Sand work for?' Jubal asked.

'He don't. But it used to be Kingsley Post,' Tolliver said.

For obvious reasons, Jubal recalled that Kingsley Post was one of the names that Billy had mentioned, but he wished he could recall the circumstance.

'Are you bringin' the sheriff in for this?' Tolliver asked Jeffs.

'It's *his* territory. Maybe he can make it here tomorrow, if you go wire him.'

'Yeah, if them Owl Creek steelheads ain't bitin',' Tolliver replied. Then he grinned unpleasantly at Jubal and went out leaving the door open behind him.

Jeffs sighed as Jubal moved to close it. 'Do you suppose young Billy could have been mistaken?' he asked.

'Yeah, I suppose,' Jubal answered. 'But that don't stop you arrestin' Sand on suspicion. I would if I was you, Marshal.'

Jeffs smiled a genuine smile. 'Yeah, but usin' your own words, *you ain't.* Besides, Tolly said he saw him in the saloon. He's my deputy, for Chris'sake.'

Jubal wasn't certain of the marshal's assessment. But it wasn't anything new. He had seen the signs before. Like it had been in New Mexico, Hirkam Jeffs was probably looking after his days until pension time.

'I reckon it's up to me to ride out an' tell Hester,' Jeffs sighed. 'I've had to do it before, but it ain't the sort o' news you get used to bringin'.'

'If it'll help, I'll ride with you,' Jubal offered.

'Thanks, but no thanks,' Jeffs responded shortly. 'You brought Billy to me, that makes it my responsibility from now on. I'll bring her back . . . she'll want to see her brother.' The marshal started to his feet, but Jubal shook his head, waved for him to remain seated.

'OK, but before you go, tell me about Ase Linder. It could be important.'

Jeffs frowned a little, eased himself back into his chair. 'Is this somethin' to do with Billy consortin' with his daughter?'

'Well, I never really knew that things had gone that far, but yeah, it might have somethin' to do with it,' Jubal admitted. 'Is she in town, do you know?'

'Iris has been gone for over a month. Ase packed her off to some fancy girls' school in Philadelphia.'

'I don't think Billy knew *that*.'

Jeffs shrugged. 'I'm guessin' he told you about him an' the old man not gettin' along, but don't waste your time thinkin' Ase would want a killin' done. The toe of a boot's more his style. Well, it would be if he could lift his leg that high. The man ain't as hale and hearty as he once was.'

'That ain't quite what Billy said, but I get your meanin'. So, how do you account for Billy gettin' shot at last year?'

'I don't, but I know he weren't the only one. There was some rustlin' in the valley at the time. Maybe it's related, maybe not. I ain't given it much thought lately.'

'So give it some now.'

'OK. What I think is, when young Billy went to Colorado, the trouble around here dried up . . . sudden like. Now the day he comes back, he gets himself shot.' Jeffs puffed out his cheeks. 'But they're facts more'n thoughts, Lorde. An' don't tell me Ase Linder's behind it.'

'How long has he lived in the valley?'

'Him an' Billy, an' Billy's sister, arrived here about the same time. That's six years ago. Ase started big an' stayed that way. After he got his ranch goin' he sent for his family, but his wife had some terminal disease an' snuffed it before they got here. Curious circumstances that left him with three kids. He sent Rex to school in Denver, an' now he's an up an' comin' lawyer. Talk is, he wants a practice back here in Pitchfork. Iris is out East, like I said, an' Esther May's managin' the ranch. It's a good family, an' Ase is a proud father.'

'Hmm. What would he be, if some young buck took a second look at one o' them daughters? Billy told me he got run off more'n once.'

'Ase was fond o' sayin' that Iris was too young to wear underlinen, let alone get married. But time passes quick out here, an' he'd have simmered down.'

Jubal took his hat off, and scratched his head. 'What's to do about Sand?' he asked.

'If he was at the saloon, like Tolly said he was, he'll be around when the sheriff gets back. Why shouldn't he be?'

'You tell *me*,' Jubal snorted. 'Or go an' ask *him*.'

'Well, I'll think about it,' the marshal returned. 'Just as long as it ain't *you*, Mr Lorde.' Jeffs gave Jubal a speculative look. 'We both know this badge I'm wearin' is only good inside town limits, so as long as I'm wearing it, I try an' stop trouble afore she starts. I'm advisin' you to hole up in the hotel tonight, not go out lookin' for trouble.'

Jubal frowned, took to a long stare at the floor. He'd often said something similar when he'd worn a badge. Now, he could see the problem from both sides, conceded that Billy didn't see that it was Sand who had fired the shot. A gut feeling for it maybe, but not copper-bottom proof. Goddamnit, at the end of the day, it wasn't enough for him to go and shoot the man. So what the hell did Billy mean?

Jubal nodded at Jeffs. 'I'll promise you one thing,' he offered. 'When the sheriff returns, I'll make sure that Sand stands trial, if nothin' else.'

'That's more like it, son. Keep it legal an' inside the town, an' I'll back you all the way,' Jeffs said, and Jubal suddenly got a different slant on the marshal.

3

After stabling the horses, Jubal purchased a shirt and a pair of denim pants. It was close to nine o'clock, and Jeffs should be back with Hester about ten. He wanted to see her; at the same time, half dreaded it.

As he now stood on the boardwalk, he heard the storekeeper locking the door behind him. He guessed he'd been an unwelcome customer, that it was already common knowledge about Billy, that Jubal was implicated in the killing. He built himself a smoke, cupped his hand against the rising wind to flick a match. Then he decided to wait at the hotel, and stepped into the main street. Halfway there, he crossed a narrow side street that housed a few honky-tonk saloons. It was where the night life centred after full dark, where the trouble started.

The Hump Rib Hotel was a two-storey, rough, clinkered construction and, like the rest of the town, looked quite deserted. But inside the lobby was brightly lit, and a clerk sat behind a desk. There was a small dining room to one side, and a stuffed buffalo's head guarded the entrance doorway to the hotel's bar.

Two men were talking near the desk. A tall girl in a green dress stood with them, but showed no interest in their conversation. She glanced at Jubal, and he took in her cascade of coppery hair, the slight movement of her lips. Her gaze brightened with sudden interest and hunger nibbled at Jubal's gut.

Then the men looked at him as he walked by them. One was a lean oldster, his ravaged face suggesting either discomfort or disdain. The other man was younger, looked more at ease, and he wore a checked suit. Jubal took him for a well-to-do merchant, a travelling salesman, perhaps.

There was no doubt they had more than a passing interest in him, Jubal thought wryly, as he passed under the bison's lifeless stare, especially the woman. The half-dozen men who were drinking at small tables, appeared to stop talking as he stepped up to the bar. A man with straw-coloured hair gave him a long, severe look before turning away.

Jubal asked the bartender for whiskey, gave an imperceptible shrug at the thought of being stared at and talked about.

After many dry weeks, he enjoyed the bite of the drink, even more so because the bottle carried a brand label. A man was entitled to this stuff in an end-of-line cow town, and he reckoned he was due. He took another look at the copper-haired woman and she gave a glossy smile. He nodded back, had a feeling that if there was a *this* time, he probably wouldn't feel cheated when it was over.

He poured himself another drink, was making a smoke, when two men entered the side door that opened on the alley.

He recognized the lanky man in the stained coat as Snoop Kirkland. The other man's great lantern jaw was unshaven, he wore a dark coat and a black hat was pushed back on his head. He stood four square on to the bar, looped his thumbs inside his belt, and scowled antagonistically. Kirkland passed behind Jubal and stopped halfway along the bar. He leaned on an elbow and grinned ingratiatingly at his associate who edged unsteadily along the bar towards Jubal.

Since he'd left the marshal's office, Jubal had been expecting some sort of confrontation, almost amused himself about how and when it would happen. Well, it's about *now*, he thought, as the scowling man edged closer to him. He could see the man's eyes were bleary with drink, and he cursed silently, took a guess at the man's identity as he shaped his cigarette paper.

'Hey, feller. I hear you been talkin' about me,' the man said thickly.

Jubal licked the cigarette paper and sealed it carefully. He was remembering how quick John Tolliver had offered an alibi for Ralph Sand, as he placed the smoke on the bar in front of him. Counted out Jeffs who could have warned Sand of what he'd said in the marshal's office.

'You hearin' me, feller? I'm Ralph Sand,' the man said.

'Is that a challenge, or a question you're puttin' up?' Jubal goaded calmly.

Jubal's manner upset Sand. His jaw dropped and he made a low, grumbling sound. Then he slapped at the side arm he was wearing. 'It's *both*, feller. *You* been sayin' it was me who shot Billy Box. *I'm* here to tell you it's a goddamn lie.'

Jubal shook his head with incredulity. It was obvious Sand had been sucking courage from a bottle. 'Where'd you get *that* from? As if I didn't know,' he asked him.

Now, blood started its rush to Sand's face. The man worked his jaw with anger. He took another move forward, slapped again at his gun, and Jubal wondered how long it would be before he drew it. It was evident the man wasn't much of a gunfighter, but you didn't have to be one of those if you had a rifle and wanted to bring down an unsuspecting man from less than fifty yards. And if it was him, he carried protection, and the alibi had already been established.

'If you *are* who you *say* you are, an' it don't look like it would be the sort o' thing you'd make up,' Jubal started, 'you got nothin' to worry about. If Billy Box was mistaken, there won't be much of a legal action against you. You could even think o' suin' for slander . . . defamation o' your sweet-natured character.'

Sand missed the insult and sarcasm. 'Huh, no need. There ain't goin' to be *anythin'* against me, feller,' he blustered. 'I'm goin' to make sure o' that.'

Jubal guessed the man was losing it, that the time had come for him to react. He turned for a quick look at Kirkland. The man hadn't moved, but Jubal didn't like the idea of him being there on his blind side. Knowing there wasn't another chance with Sand, he took a short step to one side, pulled his own Colt, and shoved the barrel firmly into the man's lower belly.

Genuine terror appeared in Sand's eyes. He started to tremble, his lips lost more colour, and his breathing seized up. In a few sobering moments, he'd seen and felt the thrust of death. Jubal was letting him take it all in.

'I can see you're a man that imagines stuff,' he said. 'Probably, what a mess your guts would make o' this floor.' Then he brought up his Colt, and cracked Sand very hard across the side of the face.

'I'm breakin' a promise, you ugly son-of-a-bitch,' Jubal muttered as, like a poleaxed steer, Sand slumped to the floor. A trickle of blood oozed from his cheekbone and ran through dark stubble. Jubal stooped to take the man's gun, but stood up to the sound of a harsh command.

'Stay out o' this,' a voice rasped out. 'Drop that gun.'

Jubal was alert and made a controlled spin around. There were two men struggling at the bar. One was Snoop Kirkland, the other was the stocky man with straw-coloured hair he'd noticed when he entered the bar.

The man had got Kirkland restrained against the bar. His big hands were wrapped tightly around the Colt that Kirkland had drawn. There was a wolfish expression on Kirkland's face and his rotten teeth were bared as he jerked a knee into the man's groin. The man groaned, but held on. He twisted Kirkland's hand viciously and cracked it against the edge of the bar. Kirkland gasped with pain, and the gun fell from his hand. The other man kicked it aside and backed off a couple of steps.

Jubal measured the situation, looked towards the man in the checked suit. He was still standing near the entrance to the bar, his features hardened, but difficult to read. Behind him stood the lady in the shiny dress. She stared at him, and he thought he detected the twitch of an impressed smile. Then he looked at Sand who was getting back to his feet. His eyes were unfocused and beneath the raw wound, muddy blood smeared one side of his face.

Jubal holstered his own gun, and in one fast movement, reached out and grabbed the man by the shirt, swung him around, hard up against the bar.

'You so much as even look at me again, I'll kill you,' he threatened icily. 'Just stay in town an' wait for the protection o' the sheriff; make a run for it an' I'll come after you. That's two ways to die quick, an' one to live a bit longer. It's a bigger choice than Billy Box had. Now, get out o' here an' make yours.'

Jubal watched to make sure Sand's legs lurched him towards the door, then he went and picked up Kirkland's gun. He walked back to the bar, stared hard at the man who was breathing hoarsely and nursing his injured fingers inside his coat.

'That makes it twice tonight you've pushed me, mister. Don't try an' get away with a third,' he warned ominously as he tossed the gun onto the bar.

'I'm takin' that,' Kirkland said, and reached out his hand.

Jubal was still holding Sand's gun. He cursed and slammed the butt of it down brutally.

Kirkland bellowed and snatched his arm off the bar. 'You smashed my goddamn thumb,' he yowled.

'Think yourself lucky you got any sort o' paw left,' Jubal sneered, and turned to the bartender. 'Hold both these Colts,' he told him. 'Keep 'em somewhere safe for Marshal Jeffs.'

Kirkland was now backing towards the entrance. 'You ain't heard the last o' this,' he seethed, through clenched teeth, and turned a shoulder through the swinging doors.

There was a whispering, murmuring silence. Some of the men had risen from their tables, looked as though they were waiting for a moment to leave.

'You let 'em both off easy, friend. Would that be your kindly nature, or a nod towards the law?' someone spoke up.

'The law, I guess,' Jubal replied and took a deep, relieved breath.

The man in the checked suit smiled, and offered Jubal his hand. Directly behind him, another man studied Jubal with thoughtful interest, but the woman wasn't in sight.

'I'm Kingsley Post,' the man said, and gripped Jubal's

hand firmly. 'Let's hope you did the right thing.'

Jubal recalled what Tolliver had told him. 'Didn't he once work for you?' he asked.

'Ralph Sand? Yeah, once. An' if I was you, I'd have my eyes an' ears ride swing for a while,' Post advised. 'Just a friendly warnin',' he added, before nodding curtly. Then he turned toward the lobby and the other man followed him out.

Jubal frowned and looked for the straw-haired man. He saw him at the end of the bar with a near empty glass in front of him. He picked up his own bottle and glass and carried them over. Without a word, he filled the man's glass, then his own.

'Must have interrupted some drinkin' time,' he suggested. 'As if you didn't know, I'm Jubal Lorde. Thanks,' he said, and chewed on a big mouthful of whiskey.

The man watched, almost looked like he had no memory of helping Jubal out. He had an open, freckle-filled face, and his eyes were clear blue. He wore a skin jerkin over a faded shirt, had trousers with patches sewn on both knees. His boots were crack worn and Jubal noticed he wasn't carrying a gun.

'I was helpin' a fellow citizen stay off a murder charge,' he answered drily.

Jubal smiled. 'Thanks anyway. Now, let me take a guess at who you might be,' he offered. 'At least what your friends might be callin' you.'

'An what might *that* be?'

'No offence, but freckles or patches?'

The man smiled back. 'None taken, an' you've obviously noticed I ain't carryin' a gun,' he said, and smiled again. 'I'm Toby Messenger. Your friend Billy Box could've mentioned me.'

'Oh yeah,' Jubal replied, putting a few of Billy's anecdotes together. He thought that Toby Messenger was a homesteader who'd been seeing Billy's sister.

'Do you reckon it was Ralph Sand who shot Billy?' the young man asked, as he twirled the whiskey in his glass.

Jubal shook his head unhelpfully. 'I don't know. I really don't. Billy said his name, that's all. I might've been makin' a hill o' beans. I've sort o' decided to let the law decide.'

Messenger put his glass on the bar. 'Nobody would've blamed you, if you'd shot him,' he said.

'Maybe, but that wouldn't have made him guilty,' Jubal replied. 'Anyways, I still might.'

'You've had your best chance,' Messenger said accusingly. 'If I'd been in your position, I wouldn't have been thinkin' about maybes or mights.'

'You would have done when the sheriff got back. You look like you got a whole lifetime ahead o' you, Toby. Why shorten it? Shootin' Sand won't bring Billy, back.'

'I know it. An' it wouldn't have been why I shot him,' Messenger started. Then he snapped a coin on to the bar. 'That's for the drink I never drunk,' he said gloomily, and tugging his hat down over his eyes he walked from the bar without another word.

Jubal looked after him, just a tad angry. But it was mostly at himself. He was that close to putting a bullet into Sand's gut, and he'd chosen to play devil's advocate. And now there was something else. They hardly knew each other, and yet Messenger had shown what amounted to an intuitive dislike for him. To Jubal's present thinking, it didn't make much sense.

He settled for his drinks and picked up his key at the

desk. He needed time to consider all that had happened since he'd arrived in town and, after exchanging a few appropriate words with the clerk, he stood for a while, thinking. He wondered if he had afforded Ralph Sand too many chances, whether he'd missed the obvious one. Then he spared a thought for Arnwood and Chase, the neighbouring ranchers whom Billy had talked into pooling their money. Each of them was owed 250 head of cattle. As he slowly climbed the stairs towards his room, he considered their whereabouts in Pitchfork.

4

On leaving the hotel bar, Kingsley Post hurriedly crossed the lobby and stepped outside. 'Who put him up to it?' he murmured, glancing up and down the dark, silent street.

'He was hittin' the bottle as soon as he got back,' the other man replied. He was Grif Benton, the man who'd followed Post from the hotel. 'When Tolliver told him what Lorde had said in the marshal's office he got worse. Snoop would've egged him on,' he added.

'He's panicky, an' I can't have him talkin' to Jeffs or the sheriff,' Post suggested.

'I know. I said he weren't to be trusted. Are we raidin' the herd tonight?' Benton asked.

'How about those men I signed on the other day? Are they teamed up with the others?'

'Yeah. An' they know better than to talk.'

'Hmm, like Sand wasn't expected to,' Post grated. 'But no, there'll be no raid tonight. Let's get on.'

Without another word, Post turned into a narrow alley, continued to where it met another that ran behind the buildings of the main street. In the deep silence, his mind returned to thoughts of Jubal Lorde. The man hadn't been spooked, and he hadn't shot anyone either. A lot of men would have killed both Sand and Kirkland for making that play, but Lorde had only roughed them up a bit. Post thought it an outcome worth remembering.

Benton suddenly stopped him by gripping his arm. They heard the sound of belligerent, raised voices out back of the hotel, and Post cursed under his breath. A fool an' his liquor, he thought. If only Lorde had shot Sand while he had the chance.

He saw the two men. Ralph Sand was sitting on the low run of steps, nursing his head. Snoop Kirkland stood over him, and his voice was low and urgent.

'Just get back there an' take him. Or *was* your guts spilled on the floor? Eh?'

Sand was muttering something, while Kirkland went on angrily. 'Go to hell,' he said finally and stomped off across the back lot toward the honky-tonks.

Sand remained a few moments longer, then he, too, took off down the alley. Benton leaned close to Post.

'He'll be goin' to sleep off his headache,' he whispered.

'Yeah. Why not make sure he does?' Post suggested.

Benton grunted his understanding, then moved off into the darkness. Post returned to the main street where he stopped at the corner and lit a cigar. A few minutes later he walked on to the edge of town, alongside a lath fence that partly screened lofty stacks of lumber. He unlocked a gate and closed it behind him, walked between a gangway of fresh-cut green pine. He inhaled the rich tang of resin, flicked his bunch of keys as he approached his log cabin of an office. Inside, he lit one of two desk lamps and dropped the stub of his cigar into a tin box. A moment later he stepped from a side door, listened, peered around then walked briskly to the back fence.

He swung two palings aside, edged through the narrow

gap and crossed a high-grassed field towards a stand of aged cottonwoods. To one side, he could see the yellow light from a lantern, then, as his eyes adjusted to the full darkness, he made out the shallow slant of a sod-roofed cabin. Then he heard the sound of a horse snickering from the annexed pole corral.

He moved forward, started when Benton drifted in beside him.

'Didn't take much to work it out,' the man whispered. 'A man has to protect his assets.'

'For Chris'sakes, they're yours too. Now you can stay here an' keep watch,' Post demanded.

Feeling less vulnerable, Post went forward until he caught the combined pungent odours of whiskey, unwashed bedding and manure. He didn't have to wait long before Sand emerged from the cabin lugging a saddle.

'Where'd you think you're goin'?' he rasped, as he stepped up behind him silently.

Sand turned his head and Post didn't wait for him to drop the saddle. He hit him with the flat of his hand, cracked it hard across the front of his repulsive features. Sand took a side step, tripped over the saddle and went sprawling into a mud drift. Post took a long hard look, and sniffed with some sort of disgust.

'Next time, I'll use my goddamn boots. You hear me, you wretched son-of-a-bitch?' he asked, with venomous hush.

'What are *you* here for?' the man whinged.

'Stop you takin' to the hills.'

'I was just clearin' out till she blows over. Ain't that what you'd want, Mr Post?' Sand sat with his back against the cabin. He was breathing hard, cradling the side of his jaw.

'I'm endin' what Lorde started,' Post explained. 'What was your idea in buckin' him?'

'I got to thinkin' what would be best, then Snoop—'

'You got to drinkin', goddamnit. Who else did you go blabbin' with?'

'No one, Mr Post, I swear it.' Sand started to push himself to his feet, but Post reached out and pushed him back down.

'I'm beginnin' to understand how someone would get a face like that,' he sneered. 'Now, tell me who you went blabbin' with?' he demanded a second time. 'Was it Bear? Did you talk to Bear Ogden?'

'I told you, Mr Post. I didn't . . . please, don't. . . .' Sand humped his back and raised his arms defensively. But Post had already turned away.

'*You* ask him. He makes me sick,' Post called out to Benton who'd made a timely appearance from the darkness. Benton moved into the wedge of pale light that fell from the open doorway of the cabin, affected a tight smirk as he reached for Sand. He hauled the frightened man to his feet and dragged him still snivelling into the cabin.

Post went to the horse, held the palm of his hand against its warm muzzle. The horse got fractious at the sounds inside the cabin, and Post made irritated noises for it to stay easy.

It wasn't long before Benton emerged, and he was holding up a few paper notes. 'All over,' he said gruffly. 'Even got back some o' the dollars you paid him.'

'Round up the boys,' Post said sharply.

'What about Lorde?'

'Never mind him. You all get back to the ranch.'

As soon as Benton had gone, Post went back to his

lumber-yard office. He extinguished the table lamp, locked up and strolled back into town. From now on, he couldn't see Lorde as a problem but, as he got closer to his saloon, he thought it would be wise to keep an eye on him. There was no telling his reaction to Billy Box's death, but Essie should be able to give him an answer to that, soon enough. He entered the doors set on the corner of the Post House saloon, for a moment stood watching the mill of his customers. A good few of the men who stood at the bar, and sat at his tables worked for him. They knew the value of keeping their mouths shut, and they didn't care much about how they earned their pay, as long as it came to them regularly. For Post, it was simply money out, then quickly back in.

He scanned the room again, saw a giant man in greasy buckskins and a ragged beard, slouched against the bar. The man was staring glumly at an empty glass, and Post watched him for a moment longer. Then he walked over to him, signalled the bartender to lift a bottle. 'On the house, Bear,' he said, addressing the massive shoulders and bull neck.

Bear Ogden moved a grubby paw towards the whiskey. He growled an appreciative noise, but Post was moving towards the pianola where he'd seen Snoop Kirkland.

'My office,' he said sharply, tapping the man's ankle with the toe of his boot.

Kirkland scowled but followed Post to the back of the saloon.

'Where's your friend Sand?' Post demanded, the moment his office door had banged shut behind them.

'Gone home, I expect,' Kirkland said, and shifted his feet uneasily. 'Huh, darn fool. I reckon he's—'

Before he could say another word, the bunch of keys

gripped tight in Post's fist caught him low in the pit of his stomach. He sank to his knees and, with his head lowered, he gasped and moaned, clutched himself with both hands. Post sat at his desk, placed the keys in a top drawer and casually opened a fat ledger.

Kirkland staggered one, then two paces backwards as he pulled himself to his feet. His face was grey; forehead sweat met with tears of pain that squeezed from his eyes. He leaned forward, licked the acid bile from his lips.

'You're a sneak . . . a pathetic weasel, Kirkland. Now, get out o' here an' don't ever come back,' Post said dully and without looking up.

Less than a minute after Kirkland had left Post's office, someone knocked. It was a halting, double tap, as though whoever it was, expected to be told to go away.

'Come in, then,' Post said offhandedly.

A small man with pinched features entered. He pushed the door gently to behind him, pulled off his hat and held it deferentially across his chest.

Post blinked his eyes and shook his head tiredly. 'Ah, Arnwood. I reckon I was just thinkin' o' you,' he said, leaning back in his chair. 'What brings you out o' the woodwork?' he added offensively.

Arnwood took a small step towards the desk. 'It's about the offer . . . the one you made me,' he started falteringly.

'What about it?'

'I want to sell. I made up my mind.'

'*You* made up your mind?' Post queried.

'I had help from my wife, if that's what you mean. We heard they got young Billy Box.'

Post took a closer look at Arnwood. 'Who'd you hear that from?' he demanded.

'Marshal Jeffs had been out to tell Hester. He stopped

by. We talked it over . . . me an' Peggy. One thing an' another, we thought it best to come an' see you straight off. You haven't changed your mind, have you, Mr Post?'

'Two hundred an' fifty head o' those cattle are yours. Is that right?' Post asked, by way of an answer.

Encouraged slightly, Arnwood nodded eagerly. 'An' I ain't lookin' for profit on 'em. I'll take what I put in. That, an' what you offered me for the place.'

'Have you mentioned that offer to anyone else?' Post asked.

'No. You said not to. Well, none except Hester. She assumed it was Ase Linder who made it. I didn't tell her no different.' Arndale grinned awkwardly.

Post stayed quiet, thoughtfully pondered on the day's doings. Things were moving. He was edging closer to the fortune he'd got earmarked.

'We want to clear from the country. So me an' Peggy won't be expectin' any shots took at us,' Arndale pursued his own fate.

'No, no,' Post replied distractedly. 'I doubt that'll happen.' The saloon keeper stared at the pages of his takings ledger, gained a few mind settling moments. He wasn't out of the woods yet. Linder was a dying man, but there was a proud young woman, and a potential county legislator, to consider. Another act of carelessness like Sands, and it was all there to lose. He offered a grim smile to Arnwood.

'It's a bad business. That ruckus between Linder an' Billy Box has got a few folk around here rattled . . . rattled about all sorts o' things. For the time bein', I reckon a deal like ours is best kept quiet.'

'Sure, Mr Post. Then it *is* a deal?' Arnwood asked hopefully.

Post nodded brusquely. 'Meet me at the bank at ten tomorrow mornin' with the deed,' he advised. He took a significant looking cigar from a box on his desk and offered it to Arnwood. 'Take a smoke on it,' he said. 'An' you remember, it's just between us.'

When Arnwood had gone, Post had some further thoughts and considerations. He had planned to raid the Colorado herd tonight, but he'd changed his mind when Tolliver brought news that Sheriff Stump was coming to Pitchfork. He stretched his shoulders, shook his head. You been bit before, he reminded himself. Right now he wasn't much further than so far so good. With his left hand, he reached for a bottle of Kentucky Bourbon; with his right, pencilled in a line of figures below a recent ledger entry. 'Yeah, so far so good,' he muttered.

5

Jubal was walking along the dimly lit hallway to his room when a narrow band of light appeared from a partly opened door. As he approached, the door opened wider and the woman in the green dress looked at him and beckoned.

'Come in,' she whispered, and stepped aside. With no specific thought in his head, Jubal pulled off his hat and stepped into her room.

The girl closed the door quietly and leaned against it, her face pale and nervous. 'I'm Essie Linder,' she said.

Jubal nodded. 'Iris's sister. Billy's friend. How'd you do,' was all he could think of.

'What was the trouble downstairs?' she asked, stepping away from the door.

'Ah, it's answers you want,' he said, with an expression of surprise and disappointment. The girl wasn't quite as pretty as he'd first thought, but she had strong, handsome features.

She returned his stare, then flushed as he looked around the room. There was a brass bedstead and a chest of drawers, a bowl and pitcher and a table and two chairs. Where rain had trickled through the shakes, the wallpaper carried patches of stain. Jubal wondered about some dresses, the amount of clothing he saw hanging in the open closet.

'I've heard a lot about you from Billy an' Hester,' she said, as if to halt his appraisal of her personal belongings. 'Are you plannin' to settle in the valley, Mr Lorde?'

'If you'd spoke to the Boxes about me, then you'll know I came here intendin' to settle,' Jubal returned. 'I know Billy wrote his sister about it. So I'm guessin' he wrote the same to *your* sister . . . Iris.'

Essie nodded. 'Yeah, he did.' she agreed. 'It's just that after what's happened, it can't be a certainty any more.'

Jubal didn't respond. He watched Essie, waited for her to say more. He wasn't sure he could trust her, and she hadn't yet said what it was she wanted to see him for.

'Did Billy ever mention me?' she asked.

'Sure he did. He said you'd be a sight for sore eyes, that distant fields always look greener. An' that's the truth.'

Essie blinked, smoothed her hands across her hips. 'Hmm, it sounds like somethin' he'd come up with, like I've only got the one dress,' she said with a sad smile. 'But you haven't answered my question about whether you're stayin'?'

'Was that here, or Pitchfork?' he asked drily.

'Pitchfork.'

'I'm stayin'.'

Essie walked to her table, idly picked at a hairbrush. 'Hester often spoke of you . . . still does. You knew her well?'

'As well as you can when you're the shoot side o' sixteen,' Jubal said. 'Why do you want to know if I'm stayin'?'

'Because Pa owns a tract of land you might be interested

in. We call it Adam's Stamp. There's good grass an' water, an' wild hay in the meadows. *That's* why I wanted to speak to you.'

Jubal considered his next question. 'An' the man I saw you with downstairs? That was your pa?'

'Yes. Ase Linder.'

Jubal nodded, thought for another moment. 'I find it mighty curious, Miss Linder, that you're more interested in sellin' me a piece o' land, than you are in Billy. Why's that so?'

What looked like a genuine expression of pain clouded Essie's face. 'That's not true,' she said. 'We all feel terrible. It's just that. . . .'

She turned away, and for a moment Jubal feared that she was about to faint. But based on what he'd seen so far, he changed his mind.

'I've heard Billy an' your pa didn't get along,' he suggested.

'That's no secret. It was to do with Iris, not personal.'

'Well, if *that* ain't personal, I'd like to know what *is*, lady,' Jubal retorted. 'Seems to me there's a few folk around here gettin' facts an' falsehoods a tad muddy.'

'Pa didn't have anythin' to do with Billy's death, if that's what you're thinkin',' she bit back.

'But it's a goddamn fact that Billy was killed today. If it turns out your pa had *anythin'* to do with it, I'll come callin',' Jubal threatened. From the assured way Essie spoke, he was hard put not to believe her. But then again, if she knew her father *was* guilty, she would almost certainly protect him. 'You heard what was said down in the lobby . . . saw what happened too. I'll learn the truth one way or another,' he added.

Essie nodded. 'I can see that. An' I'm *not* more

interested in sellin' you the Stamp,' she said, with more control. 'I intended askin' you when I first heard you were comin' back with the herd. We've got trouble in the valley, an' Hester's goin' to need help now that Billy's dead.'

Jubal frowned. He recalled Hester's remark about him sorting out any trouble, felt an immediate stab of guilt.

'It was only a few hours ago that Billy was shot. What's so urgent about me buyin' your land? Assumin' I had that kind o' money, which I don't.'

'I'd give you a lease on it,' she said, quickly.

'You'd thought that out too, had you?' Jubal said. 'Where does your pa figure in this?'

Essie shook her head. 'He doesn't. I'll tell him when I'm ready.'

'Why are you wantin' to sell? Are you actin' on his behalf?'

'I've had power of attorney for a year. For *why*? Well, maybe I want to surprise him. Maybe we're in debt an' need the money. What difference does it make to you?'

Jabal gave her a steady look. 'You're nibblin' around the edges, lady,' he said. 'I don't generally look for trouble, but when I'm in it, I like to know what got me there.'

'Will you at least consider takin' a lease on the Stamp?' she appealed.

'I'd have to see the land first. See just how much trouble it's worth.' Jubal gave a wry undertaking to Essie. He thought her appeal was convincing, if not its reason. It had fleetingly crossed his mind before, but now he thought it even more unlikely that Ase Linder had paid Ralph Sand to do his killing. Billy chasing after his daughter was too slight a motive.

'I can show you the land in a day or two,' the girl

assured him. 'Once you see it, I'm sure we can do business.'

'Yeah, I'm sure.' Jubal recalled Billy saying it would make a man whistle. 'Do you know if Arnwood an' Chase are in town?' he asked.

'I haven't seen them. Me an Pa drove in late this afternoon,' she explained. 'He had a fall last winter. Since then, he's been seein' the doc, regular. He prescribes somethin' for the pain.'

'I heard it was a bad one . . . the winter. You all lost a lot o' stock.'

Essie nodded. 'Most o' the smaller outfits did well to last through. Even now they're just hangin' on.' She hesitated, then added bitterly, 'I know one rancher who would have sold out weeks ago, if Hester hadn't talked him out of it.'

'Do you mean Dudley Arnwood?'

She looked surprised. 'Yes. How did you know?'

'Hester wrote Billy about it, just before we left Colorado. He sent Arnwood a letter tellin' him to hang on until we got through with the cattle.' Jubal paused for thought. 'Who was it wanted to buy Arnwood out?' he asked.

'I don't know,' Essie, said. 'It was just a rumour.'

No, she's lying, Jubal thought. She's lying because for some reason she's afraid to tell me. 'Whoever it was, I don't suppose they liked the idea o' Hester Box pokin' her nose in. That's about it, don't you think?'

'I really wouldn't know.'

'Like hell you wouldn't,' Jubal rasped. 'I ain't always been the sharpest knife in the drawer, but I'm keen enough to know there's a lot o' stuff you ain't tellin' me.' With that, he reached out and grabbed her wrist, quickly pulled her close. 'Now why should I buy a piece o' land that I ain't seen yet, from someone I don't know yet?' he demanded harshly. 'An' this time, don't tell me you don't know.'

'Let go of me, damn you,' she cursed. She swung her hip against his, tried to wrench her arm free. She breathed hoarsely, through bared teeth. 'I said, let go of me.'

The closeness shook Jubal. For the shortest moment, his awareness of her as a woman took his mind off his predicament. He also knew that he wasn't going to make her reveal more than she already had. He released his grip slowly, picked up his hat and went to the door.

'Jubal,' Essie said.

He turned and saw the curious, restless smile that moved across her face. It wasn't quite supporting what she'd just told him. Two impulsive strides back into the room brought him to her, and his mouth pressed determinedly on to hers.

'I don't know if that's what you wanted,' he said, when they broke away, but unless you change your mind an' let me in, there'll likely be more o' the same.'

'I *will*, but not now,' she responded. 'Trust me, it's very important, an' please tell no one you've seen me. Can you do that, Jubal?'

Cursing inwardly, Jubal stood in the upper hallway again. Frustrated, he dragged at the brim of his hat, considered paying one of the honky-tonks a visit. Then he checked his stemwinder, realized that the marshal should be back with Hester.

When he reached the lobby, the clerk was taken aback and gave him a surprised double look.

'The marshal was here a while ago lookin' for you,' the man accused from behind his desk. 'You weren't in your room.'

'Smoke an' mirrors,' Jubal flipped back and walked straight from the hotel.

Kingsley Post had just finished appraising his ledger entries when John Tolliver pushed into his office.

'You got to hear this,' the deputy started.

'No, *you* hear *this*,' Post snapped back. 'Next time you come in here, knock, understand?'

Tolliver rolled his eyes, gave an irked smile and backed out through the door. He knocked and came in again.

'What the hell is it, smart ass?' Post demanded.

'Beg to report, sir, Ralph Sand's been killed, an' the marshal's arrested Jubal Lorde,' Tolliver said glibly.

Post worked his jaw, slowly shut his ledger. 'How, when?' he questioned flatly.

'I was makin' my rounds . . . thought to go an' ask him about that scrap he had with Lorde. Damn near tripped over him. He was inside the doorway . . . knifed an' cold dead.'

'Where's Jeffs now? Is he in town?'

'Yeah. He went to the undertaker's with the Box girl an' Toby Messenger. He stopped by the hotel to get Lorde on account o' the girl wantin' to see him. The clerk said Lorde was up in his room, but he weren't, an' Hirk couldn't find him. The girl didn't want to be on her own, so Messenger takes her on to the minister's house.'

'What about Lorde?'

'I'm comin' to it,' Tolliver said tetchily. 'Me an' Hirk was at the office, when in he walks. Hirk asked him where he'd been, an' he said in his room. Hirk called him a liar, said he'd warned him to keep away from Sand.'

'How did Lorde react?'

'He didn't . . . just listened. Hirk put it to him, that after the row at the Hump Rib, he went up to his room all right, but went right on down the back steps to trail Sand. Out at the cabin, he stuck him.'

'An' Lorde still didn't react?'

Tolliver shook his head. 'No, he was real peaceable, just swore he'd never left the hotel. But Hirk knew he *hadn't* been in his room. Funny thing is, Mr Post, he *was* sort o' convincin',' he added.

Post looked as though he didn't understand what was going on. 'All right,' he said. 'If Sheriff Stump arrives here tomorrow, I want you here as well. OK?'

'Yeah, OK. Everythin' workin' profitably, is it, Mr Post?' Tolliver said, and grinned deviously.

'What do you mean?'

Tolliver shrugged. 'Hell, it's only jawbone. But I was thinkin' that from a storeroom in piss alley, you now got *this* place, the lumber yard, *an'* a fat ranch. In a couple o' years, you made out real good, Mr Post. Yessir, *real* good.'

Post's manner hardened. He waited for Tolliver to continue; when he didn't, he said frostily, 'Is that *all*, Deputy?'

'I'd like to know when *I* get to make somethin',' Tolliver replied. 'My hide's involved in this as much as yours.'

'Well, not quite. But you're gettin' paid well enough,' Post said.

'Tonight's raid could've been risky for all of us. Could've put an end to everythin'.'

Post controlled a rise of impatient anger. 'When a man wants somethin' bad enough, he ought to take a chance on gettin' it,' he said calculatingly. 'You use that badge o' yours for a kick-back every chance you get, Deputy,' he rasped. 'We're just playin' at different tables. Now get out o' here, an' keep quiet.'

When Tolliver had gone, Post circled his office with a fresh cigar clenched between his teeth. He too, was now wondering where Jubal Lorde had got to, suddenly sensed a cold sweat between his shoulder blades. Since learning the truth about Ase Linder, he hadn't made a move without seeing the place he was going, hadn't asked a question without knowing the answer. Now this stranger from Colorado threatened to become a burr under his saddle. It wouldn't be the first time a man had lied about being in or out of a hotel room, but Post wanted to know where he was, not where he wasn't.

But when Lorde did become a real problem – as Ralph Sand had done – he'd do something about it.

6

Jubal lay on his cot smoking a cigarette. Morning sounds came through the high barred window, the creak of a wagon wheel, someone shouting, the quick bark of a pariah dog. It was Pitchfork awakening to another day.

He took a last drag, flicked the butt end on to his breakfast tray and sat up. He wondered how long it would be before Essie Linder came forward to clear him. Until then, he'd be keeping his promise to her, and remain silent. Then he thought about how he'd handle it if she didn't.

He swung his legs to the ground and got to his feet when he heard a door open. It was Hirkam Jeffs who peered through the bars at Jubal.

'Made up your mind about last night?' he asked gruffly.

Jubal shrugged. 'I've already explained,' he said. 'I wouldn't be here right now, if you'd gone along with what I told you about Sand.'

'He had an alibi.'

'Did you check?' Jubal demanded. 'Hell no, you just took the word o' someone who's more interested in scrapin' muck from his fingernails. Who hired him, anyhow?'

'Town fathers. Same as hired me, as well you know,' Jeffs said. 'Anythin' else you want to say?'

'Yeah. Sand tried to gull me last night, but it didn't work. He was runnin' scared, an' it's as plain as your face, he was killed to keep him from talkin'.'

'That's as maybe, feller.' Jeffs then turned the key in the cell door. 'This don't mean you're gettin' out,' he said. 'I'm bein' real lenient, 'cause Hester Box has asked to see you. You owe her that, at least.'

The marshal's office door was ajar, and a hollow feeling hit Jubal in the pit of his stomach the moment he saw Billy's sister. But she wasn't on her own. Toby Messenger was leaning inside the outer door, and he lifted a hand to conceal his voice when he said something to her.

When they turned towards him, Jubal noted that whatever Messenger had said, it had angered Hester. But when she saw him, the anger vanished and her eyes brightened.

'Jubal,' she said simply and took a step towards him.

Jubal held out his hands to take hers. 'I'm sorry,' he said. 'I'd have come straight off, but the marshal said no. I'm real sorry about everythin'.'

The outer door slammed shut and Jubal looked past Hester to see that Messenger had gone. Then he smiled at Hester, noted that she featured Billy, the same long, blonde hair.

'They killed him, Jubal,' she sobbed in a small voice. She moved her hands to grip his arms, searched his face with eyes that suddenly turned hard. 'Billy never hurt anyone, but they killed him. I'm glad, glad you did what you did, Jubal.'

Jubal took a short moment, then blinked with amazement.

'We'll get you out o' this.' Hester whispered fiercely. 'As soon as I leave here, I'm goin' to see J.J. Patch. He's a real good lawyer.'

Jubal groaned, cursed inwardly. Hester was thinking he'd killed Sand. 'Hold up here, Hester. I reckon you've got this wrong,' he answered back. 'The thought's a fine one, but it ain't true. It weren't *me* who killed him.'

'Then *who*, Jubal? Marshal Jeffs, said that—'

'Yeah, I can guess what the marshal said.' With that, Jubal ushered Hester into a chair. 'But I'll tell you somethin',' he continued. 'Just listen, an' think about it.'

After Jubal had explained about the happening in the rainy pass, Hester pressed her fingers to her top lip that trembled uncontrollably. 'He wanted you to sell out, Hester. That's what he said you was to do . . . for me to tell you.'

Hester shook her head stubbornly. 'Last thing I'll do.'

Jubal gave a doubtful, but understanding frown. 'Do you know anythin' about runnin' a ranch?' he asked.

'Enough,' she responded defiantly. 'We made out while Billy was away.'

'Who's *we*?' Jubal asked.

'Frank Pinner's our top hand. Him an' Wes Drayton will stick by me.'

Jubal nodded. 'The herd should be pushed into the valley today,' he said. 'Marshal let me write this,' he added and handed over a folded sheet of paper. 'I want you to see Bull McRae gets it.'

Hester tucked the note into a side pocket, then explained how last night, Wes Drayton had ridden to tell Arnwood and Chase about Billy's death.

'They're due in town this mornin'. Chase will have his two sons with him,' she said.

Jubal had a closer look at Hester, saw the puffiness, around her red-rimmed eyes. It was the result of her private tears. But he knew of her stubborn streak, believed she would survive the hardship.

'I've heard local trouble mentioned, Hester. Do you have any idea who's behind it?' he asked.

'Toby thinks . . . well, most people think it's ol' Ase Linder.'

'But *you* don't,' Jubal suggested.

Hester shook her head. 'I thought it was goin' to be so different, Jubal,' she said ruefully. 'We have so much to talk about.'

'There'll be time,' he replied. 'An' don't go botherin' that attorney feller. I doubt I'll need him. Oh, an' it's important that Bull McRae's told I'm delayed. I'd hate to think what the trail crew would do to this town if they find out I'm in jail.'

Hester looked into Jubal's dark eyes. 'There's somethin' you're not tellin' me,' she said. Impulsively, she put her arms around his neck and kissed him on the side of his mouth. 'But you will,' she added, before huskily whispering goodbye.

Within moments of Hester hurrying from the office, the door opened behind Jubal and the marshal's gruff voice called for him.

Back in the cell, Jubal built a cigarette. He thought about, then settled on a reason for Toby Messenger's continued resentment. He knew the man had been seeing a lot of Hester, and she'd likely told him all about Jubal Lorde from Colorado. That was it then. The freckle-faced homesteader was jealous. He was also capable of putting a bullet into Ralph Sand. He'd told Jubal as much the previous evening.

Jubal struck a match, held up the small flame. Straight from release, he'd go looking for Snoop Kirkland. Roughing him up for some answers would be well-earned. He dropped the spent match and cursed his burnt finger. Then he stretched out on his cot and wondered how long it would be before Essie Linder learned of his arrest, what she would do about it.

In her room at the Hump Rib Hotel, Essie stared angrily at her reflection in the mirror. She was trying to reason things out, but she couldn't and was justly frustrated. Jubal had told her it wasn't true, but she still heard a small voice of conscience telling her she had been an unwitting party to Billy's murder. She couldn't believe that Kingsley Post would go to such lengths to get what he wanted, and she had no proof. But the chances of him being involved filled her with cold, rational fear. She desperately wanted to rid herself of him, and for that, she needed Jubal's help, even if he didn't yet trust her.

Leaving her room she went to the door at the end of the hall and opened it quietly. Her father was still asleep. Yesterday's events had exhausted him, and his appearance shocked her. His face was grey, his breathing was shallow and a slight, veined hand hung over the edge of the bed. She recalled his fall last winter, the complaint of pains and how they grew steadily worse. Day by day she had watched the flesh shrink from his bones and it hurt and upset her.

Ase Linder's eyes blinked open and he turned his head to look at her. 'I ain't dead yet. But what's left o' my life, I'm sure sleepin' away,' he grumbled. He squinted through the window at the sun that warmed the rumpled bed covers. 'That big ol' lantern hardly ever beat *me* out o' bed.'

'Times change, Pa,' Essie said and smiled warmly. She kissed his cheek and fluffed the pillow around his bony shoulders. She took a step back when she saw he was watching her very closely.

'What is it?' she asked. 'Why are you lookin' at me like that?'

'You been actin' funny o' late. I'm thinkin' you're hankerin' for somethin'.'

Essie grinned. 'That could be true o' most folk who live around here,' she said frivolously.

'It's time you was married, Essie,' he said quietly. 'I thought you an' Kingsley Post were . . . well. . . .'

She flushed, made puffy noises and turned away. It was true that when Post first came to the valley, she had stepped out with him. They had gone to the roundabout dances, but she'd never really liked him, or held any feeling for him. And it had stayed that way until he divulged what he knew about her father, the way he'd used the information to crook her into his needs. Then she'd hated him. She hadn't dare speak up and, with her indirect help, he'd grown to become a power in the valley.

'I know he's a pushin' man, Essie,' Linder said. 'Not the most attractive trait, I know, but he gets things done.'

'I'll get my man when I see him, Pa. He'll be someone who'll want more for his kids than he's had for himself,' Essie replied.

'Yeah, I follow your drift. Just make damn sure he is a man,' Linder advised earnestly. 'You hear what happened to Ma Hogan? Huh, after producing a brood o' snot noses, turns out her husband was a goddamn heifer brand.'

'For Chris'sake's, Pa,' Essie snapped back. 'Bein' stove up sure hasn't improved the nicety o' your mind.'

'Watch your language, daughter. An' heed what I say.'

'I will, Pa. Meantime the ranch don't run itself.'

'I know, I'm only teasin' you, Essie,' he said. 'I know you got reasons for not likin' Post, but why are you against him buyin' the Stamp? I hate seein' all that good grass goin' to waste. It ain't as if we don't need the cash, an' that ain't blame for the loss o' minin' stock,' he added in a considerate and kindly way.

'I know, Pa, but I did,' Essie replied. 'I was sayin' to Hester that we might lease. She told me that Jubal Lorde will need land if he stays in the valley.'

'Is he willin' to lease?'

'I'm goin' to see him an' find out. But right now, I'll see about some breakfast. You must eat.'

'Bring me a goddamn bottle,' he said, and closed his eyes. 'Eatin's for them who tie handkerchiefs to their arms at barn dances.'

'An' then I'm goin' to see about gettin' you into one o' them rest homes up in Montana,' she answered back, as she left the room.

She walked slowly to the other end of the hallway, for a few minutes stood thoughtfully looking from a window. She watched impassively as, on the opposite side of the street, Hester talked with Toby Messenger.

The next time she saw her friend was after she'd partaken of a dull, meaningless breakfast. She had set out to find her, but was no further than the boardwalk outside of the hotel. This time, Hester was alone, and had come from the town marshal's office. Essie hesitated. Still lodged at the back of her mind was the dismal thought that her friend would consider her father to be in some way responsible for the death of her brother Billy.

'Hester, I'm so terribly sorry,' Essie said, after gathering courage to cross the street. 'People are talkin', sayin' so many awful things. I didn't know how to . . . you know.'

Hester offered a drained smile. 'It's all right, I understand,' she accepted, and the girls enjoyed a tentative embrace.

'Thank you. Is there anythin' I can do?' Essie asked.

Hester shook her head sadly. 'Me an' Pastor Weems made most of the arrangements last night. The funeral's ten o'clock tomorrow.'

'Doesn't seem much, does it?' Essie said, but she wasn't seeking an answer. 'Pa will want to be there,' she added.

There was an awkward moment, and the girls watched a rig pass by, a bunch of riders raising dust at the far end of the street.

It was Hester who broke the short silence. 'That would be good. I haven't seen him for a while,' she said, without any obvious side or inference.

Moments later, the five riders who'd entered town pulled rein in front of them. It was Owen Chase and his sons, and they were with Frank Pinner and Wes Drayton. The men touched their hats, and Chase eyed Essie with dry interest.

'We stopped by for Dudley Arnwood, but his wife said he got up early to tally his stock,' Pinner said.

'He won't be needed,' Hester told him, and handed over Jubal's note. Pinner read it and frowned.

'Where *is* Jubal? Why ain't he ridin' with us?' he asked.

'He's been delayed . . . be along later.' Hester went along with Jubal's wishes, didn't say any more until after the horseman had ridden away.

'Pa an' me were just talkin' about Jubal Lorde,' Essie said. 'I've been thinkin' I might ask him if he'd be interested in takin' a lease on our land.'

Hester bit her bottom lip and shook her head. 'He's in

jail, Essie. They're sayin' that last night he killed Ralph Sand – the man Billy claimed shot him. But he wouldn't . . . couldn't. He was at the hotel.'

Knowing what she did, and confronted with Hester's clear-cut defence of Jubal, Essie quickly guessed the truth of what must have happened out at Sand's cabin. She also knew she'd have to go and tell Hirkam Jeffs that it was *her* hotel room that Jubal Lorde had been in. The marshal wouldn't say anything, so there was no reason why Kingsley Post should ever learn of her meeting.

Face to face with Hester, Essie found the half truths and deceit difficult to handle. She found herself hurrying along the street, troubled at the way Hester had looked at her when she had apologized for moving on so hurriedly.

7

Kingsley Post was in his yard office, ordering lumber from Rockford. Freight charges were increasing, and as a consequence he'd been thinking of building his own saw mill. With more settlers coming into the valley, it wouldn't be long before the railroad built a spur line out to Pitchfork. Then the town would be well connected, shipping as far north as the Yellowstone and Billings, Montana.

'You an' your goddamn knockin',' was Tolliver's first bluster on entering Post's office. 'You'll forget protocol when you hear this lot.'

'What's goin' on?' Post demanded.

'Lorde's out o' jail, an' Essie Linder's told Hirk that it was him in her room at the hotel,' the deputy marshal said breathlessly. 'He's been to every goddamn spit an' sawdust house in town, an' I mean every one. I'm wonderin' if it was Snoop Kirkland who killed Sand, 'cause that's who he was lookin' for.'

Post's eyes narrowed and he cursed. It was Lorde visiting Essie that interested him; what had passed between them? He cursed again, knew he'd have to see Essie to find out. 'Did Lorde find him?' he asked.

Tolliver shook his head. 'No. Kirkland kept the doors swingin' last night. He ended up sleepin' with the horses at the stable. Strange, 'cause he's usually too miserly to get roostered.'

But it wasn't strange to Post. Kirkland was still nursing his hurt feelings, now frightened that Lorde was looking for him. Unlike Sand, Kirkland hadn't said anything so far, but Lorde would make him. That was a dead certainty, and a lot more for Post to worry about.

'Is Lorde in town?' he asked Tolliver.

'No. He picked up his horse an' headed out. I hear they're pushin' the herd through this mornin'.'

Post nodded slow and meaningful. It meant the trail hands would probably get paid off this afternoon, and that Lorde would come to town with them. Odds on, that he would continue looking for Kirkland.

'Find Bear,' he said. 'Tell him to be out back o' the saloon at first dark. But first, get hold o' Kirkland an' tell him I want to know where they're pushin' that herd. An' tell him to keep out o' sight. You got that?'

Tolliver grinned. 'Yeah. If he does spot Lorde, he'll likely darken his pants.'

An hour later, Post stepped down from his rig, at the far end of town. He lifted his hat, smiled at Essie Linder.

'Nice mornin' for a drive,' he offered suggestively.

'Then go for one,' she said sharply and walked on.

Within a couple of steps Post was nudging her close. 'You're comin' with me. I've a few things to say.'

Essie looked at him and he caught the glimmer of fear in her eyes. Then it was gone and an expression of blunt loathing took its place. But she didn't protest further, and he led her compliantly back to the rig.

'I do believe if you were carryin' a pistol beneath them skirts, I'd be kissin' dirt by now,' he said belligerently.

They rode from town, both wrapped in their own thoughtful silences. When they were nearly a mile out, Essie was the first to speak.

'Where are we goin'?' she asked.

'Someplace where you tell me what you an' Jubal Lorde have to say to each other,' he said. 'You can make that place right here an' now if you like.'

'Ah, that's it. You think I'm arrangin' some payback,' she responded. 'Well, sorry, Mr Post, that's a move for blackmailin' low life, like *you*.'

'We had a deal, Essie,' Post sniffed. 'Your business is my business. What we know's just between us, an' if you want it to stay that way, we keep quiet. If you're thinkin' there's any honourable ground, remember, there ain't much difference between what your pa did, an' what I'm doin'.'

'What my pa did, he did by himself,' Essie snapped back. 'He didn't pay anyone to do it for him. He had a family to support; there was no other choice. He took that money from a business that could afford it, an' he paid it all back. After our ma died, he bought the ranch, worked at it an' made money to get us all started. He never took one penny for himself. Every dollar he earned since was earned lawfully. It was for our futures an' our family's futures, until *you* took it. But o' course you know all that,' she added bitterly.

'Well, it's still your family name you got to consider, Essie. If you don't care about yourself, think o' *them* . . . your sister . . . that upstandin' legal eagle brother.'

'Whatever happens to us, Kingsley, you'll never be more than someone who sucks at scum,' she seethed.

'Nice ladylike turn o' phrase, Essie May. Sounds like

you're sinkin' already.'

'You're the sort who makes folk have them thoughts . . . say them things.'

It took a moment, but Essie's words stung Post. 'I'm an ambitious man, an' if I have to sup with the devil an' use people to get what I want, I will,' he retaliated. He drew the rig to a halt. 'What was Lorde doin' in your room?' he asked once again.

'If I was doin' with Jubal Lorde what you think I was doin', you'd be dead by now,' she said jadedly.

Post snorted angrily. He took Essie's knee in an iron-hard grip, pinched tight against the side of her kneecap. 'If you don't want to crawl back to town, tell me,' he commanded.

The intense pain burned into the top of Essie's leg. 'OK,' she gave in. 'He heard about the tract we call Adam's Stamp . . . asked me about takin' a lease on it. He needs land . . . wants to stay on.' It wasn't quite the truth, but Essie thought it was enough to protect herself from more hurt.

Post released the pressure from her knee. 'Well, if that's the truth of it, that's good for you. If not, this is me bein' real neighbourly. Either way, Jubal Lorde won't be buyin' land or anythin' else from you.'

The man flicked the reins, called for his rig horse to turn. He looked sideways at his anguished, miserable passenger.

'Remember, your ol' man might have paid the money back, but he ain't ever paid for the crime,' he persisted. 'How'd you reckon he'd survive a few years in the State Pen?'

Essie didn't answer. All she knew was, she would do anything to keep Post from carrying out his threat to her father, to ruin her family. As for the money lost in the mining-stock collapse, it wasn't true. Essie had invested the family savings in Kingsley Post when he'd threatened to go public about her father. By sheer ill fortune, Post had encountered her brother, Rex, in Denver. The young man who'd just graduated from law school had got maudlin drunk and confessed that his father had stole $1,000 from the North-West Stage Line, where he'd worked as a stage driver. And Post had remembered the name. He'd used it to blackmail Essie when he made the connection on returning to Pitchfork.

Many times since, Essie had considered a way to silence the man. The difference now was, she didn't revile herself quite so much for it.

After his unsuccessful search for Snoop Kirkland, Jubal rode from town toward the pass. His sense of freedom on being released from jail was soon gone, and wilful anger had taken its place. Essie Linder had gotten him out of jail all right, but he hadn't seen her. He would, of course, for Jubal guessed she knew plenty about the valley's trouble.

Approaching the slopes of the pass, Jubal picked out the horseman topping the ridge. The rider was followed by a solid wedge of cattle that thickened and spread, before spilling down the slope. Then he saw the flanking riders as he spurred to meet Bull McRae. The trail boss was riding point, and Jubal lifted a hand in greeting.

'No shortage o' good grass here, Bull.'

'It's a sight,' McRae agreed. 'Young Billy weren't far wrong.'

'He said it makes a man whistle,' Jubal recalled wistfully.

They rode on stirrup to stirrup, and McRae squinted at

Jubal. 'You been fightin' in that town?' he asked with a tight smile.

'Might've been,' Jubal admitted. As they rode, he told McRae of the trouble, but excluded the bit with Essie Linder.

McRae appraised Jubal with his shrewd eyes. 'But you're stayin'.' he said.

Jubal nodded. 'Yeah, you bet. You want to work for me, Bull?'

McRae nodded back. 'Sure. How many of us do you need?'

'Two. We'll pay the others off this evenin'.'

At the sound of running horses, both men turned in their saddles.

'Frank Pinner an' Owen Chase,' McRae said.

The four men sat their horses while McRae introduced Jubal. Hester's top hand was a solid-looking man, and he fixed Jubal with an open, steady gaze.

'Has the sheriff come in yet?' Chase asked.

'Jeffs thinks the mornin', but then again, maybe this afternoon,' Jubal told him.

'Yeah, well, I'm goin' to feel a lot better when we get the cows on to our grass,' Chase said, and rose in the saddle to sweep his arm towards the north-west. 'Me an' Dudley Arnwood an' Hester are all backed up against the Copper Hills. There's a natural little basin up there where we can tally brand. We won't have to worry about gettin' jumped either.'

Jubal frowned. 'Seems funny that none o' you got any real idea who's shakin' the law.'

'That's 'cause we're dealin' with some goddamn hoodoo,' Pinner said. 'Little pinches o' cattle get rustled an' the Lord only knows where they end up. A feller even gets a shot taken at him an' there's no sign of a shooter.' He shook his head. 'So it beats me. Some are accusin' ol' Ase Linder, but I ain't so sure.'

'Does Post keep to his side of the fence?' Jubal asked.

'Post's all right,' Chase put in. 'We ain't had no truck with him, if that's what you mean.'

They rode on, and Chase pointed out where the ranches were located. 'Linder's Rod 4's up along those south ranges. Graze an' water stretches for ten miles. On the other side o' that shoulder's the tract they call Adam's Stamp,' he explained. 'For anyone who goes fishin', there's big steelheads up in the hills, but it's rough country. There's some nesters, maybe half-a-dozen stump farms, but they're well scattered.'

'Is Post's spread around here?' Jubal wanted to know.

'Yeah, east o' the Stamp.'

'An' Toby Messenger? How about him?'

'He's below us, down along Black Sage Crick,' Frank Pinner said. 'Toby's had some tough luck. Last winter just about finished him. He lost most of his stock an' crops.'

'Yeah, we all had our troubles,' Chase agreed. 'But maybe times are changin'.' He glanced back at the herd and grinned. 'I'm damn glad our cows got here. A man with cattle can get credit when he needs it. Are you goin' to tell us the whys an' wherefores o' Billy gettin' shot?' he directed at Jubal.

For the next few minutes, Jubal gave them a sketchy account of the shooting as they rode. He didn't want to say too much. On their own admission there were only banshees and shadows to fight. But a word of incitement from Jubal, and they would ride as a wound-up lynch party.

All day they rode, and with the sun lowering, they pushed the herd towards the copper-coloured hills. Jubal's gaze swept the steep sides of the natural basin, the studded boulders, the cedars and scrub oak. The hills beyond were scoured by centuries of wind and rain, scarcely anything grew in its low slopes of gritty soil. Crude brush fences had blocked off two gashes in the basin and the crew stretched another across its narrowest entrance.

Later, after dusk, when the men were readying themselves for going into town, Jubal called Daniel and Erskine Crane to one side. They were cousins, two 'punchers he'd been keeping an eye on as possible ranch hands. He asked if they would be interested in steady work with him, and they had said yes. Then he had a word with Chase, who, with his sons and Wes Drayton, would remain as night hawks.

On the ride into Pitchfork, Jubal decided he'd continue his search for Snoop Kirkland. But this time he would find him, beat information out of him, if he had to. Other than that, he could only imagine the possibilities for trouble that awaited him and his crew.

8

It was full dark by the time they reached town and swung down in front of the Hump Rib Hotel. Hester greeted them from the veranda, then she led the crew inside to a small swag-curtained side room.

'Arnwood still owes his share of the wages. I wonder why he didn't show?' Hester said afterwards, when she and Jubal had paid the men off. She gave a tired smile at Jubal's shrug. 'Yeah, you're right. I guess we'll see him tomorrow. Right now, I'm more interested in a meetin' with sweet Mr Morpheus.'

'Come on then. I'll walk you to the pastor's house.'

Hester scooped what remained of the payout money into her duster purse. Jubal made a cigarette as he watched her, but he was thinking of Essie May. He wondered if she was up in her room, right now.

It was an intensely dark night, for the clouds had drifted in on a cold breeze from the Wind River mountains. For comfort, and a measure of support, Hester tucked her arm through Jubal's, pressed it against her until they stopped in front of the Weems' residence.

'You can let go now, if you want,' he said and smiled.

'I was just steerin' you away from the jail. We don't want

you spendin' another night in there,' she replied, adding some to her returned smile.

Jubal waited until she had gone inside. He knew the spark wasn't there, not *that* spark anyhow, and he felt ill at ease about it. 'Goddamn it,' he said almost aloud. 'I'm goin' to have to hurt her again.'

Discordant waves of shouting and pianola music welcomed Jubal to the lane of honky-tonks and dog-hole bars. He fended off an excited cowboy who was stomping the boards even before he'd pushed through the first set of batwings.

'I'm gettin' me a real hump tonight,' the man sneered. 'Somethin' that beats a goddamn saddle horn.'

'Just keep your head down,' Jubal muttered an optimistic bit of advice to himself, as he entered the bawdy saloon. From beneath his droopy hat brim, his dark eyes quartered the room. He saw two of the paid-off crew drinking at the near end of the bar and tentatively raised his hand.

'Hey, Jube, you want a drink?' one of them called out.

'Thanks. But I'm lookin' for Dummy an' McRae. You seen 'em?'

'Last I seen, they was headed towards that saloon on the corner.'

Jubal nodded that he understood, and he told them he'd go over there. 'If you run out o' money, I'll be at the hotel later,' he added.

Outside, he cut diagonally across the street, through yellow slabs of light that chopped erratically from windows, through swinging doors. Outside of the Post House, a drunk was waving his arms about. He was making nonsensical threats, and a horse at the hitch rack threw its head up in annoyance.

Jubal stepped around the rack, was up on to the boardwalk before he realized there was no spirited or comparable noise spreading from Kingsley Post's saloon.

Expressions of discretion and valour passed through his mind as he eased cautiously through the double swing doors. A dozen cowhands cluttered one end of the bar; the Crane cousins and Bull McRae stood at the other. In between, a great hulk of a man held Dummy Parsons firmly up against the bar, and with one great maw was slapping the side of his head.

'Wonder what the hell's got into Bear,' someone near Jubal muttered. 'Mr Post usually uses him to stop trouble, not start it.'

'Must've been tyin' one on with the rotgut. An' that's a fight no one wins,' another voice added. 'He'll likely give that ol' feller brain damage.'

'Well, if that's so, he sure ain't from around here,' the first man wisecracked back and they both laughed.

The voices drew the big man's attention and Jubal caught the fearful sight of deep-set glittering eyes in a big hair-covered face.

'Was you meanin' to crowd me? I don't like bein' crowded,' the man rumbled out, as he turned back to Dummy.

'Like a goddamn mouse to cheese,' Jubal muttered, as his vitals gripped at a silent, far-off warning. Why should this man start bullying the old camp cook the very moment he stepped into the saloon? He cursed and threw a quick look at McRae. The trail boss gave a slight shake of his head, held up his hand as if to wait a moment.

'You'll have to take some learnin' in how not to crowd,' the big man said, and lifted a heavy knee into Dummy's stomach. 'Should be more room now,' he went on, as Dummy gasped and slid to the floor.

'Hey fatso!' Jubal called out. 'You're carryin' a gut so big, a feller would have to be out in the street so's not to crowd you.'

Bear Ogden looked slightly puzzled, as he turned to confront Jubal. 'Who the hell are you? This ain't your fight,' he scowled.

'I'm his friend,' he answered and nodded at Dummy. 'An' I *am* crowdin' you.'

'Take him an' all, Bear,' somebody said. 'Break him open.'

Dummy scrambled away, as other men backed off. Others heaved themselves up on to the bar to watch.

Jubal unbuckled his gunbelt and tossed it to Bull McRae as he quickly took in the situation. The big man appeared to have more than a hundred pounds advantage and topped him by half a foot. Ogden moved ponderously into some space. With his legs spread and massive shoulders hunched, he peered more closely at Jubal. It was as though he'd found something new to contend with – a kitten and a fat, summer bee.

Having learned something of bare-knuckle fighting while scouting for the army, Jubal stepped forward to meet him. He smiled icily before smashing a tightly balled fist into Ogden's nose, gritted his teeth before swinging a left, hard into the body. It was like hitting a steer between the horns, and he unleashed another right into the man's bunched shoulder muscles. The big man reacted as the steer might have. Completely ignoring the body blows, he snorted a bit and tossed his shaggy head.

Jubal knew there wasn't any way to hurt the man without breaking some hand bones. But he smashed

Ogden again on the nose. This time he drew some blood, but the man's nose was already flat, the bridge a broad lump that could soak up punches. Ogden grinned unthinkingly and stomped forward. He pawed at Jubal's fists, turned tight circles, sensing for range. He swung a looping right hand that Jubal ducked under to smash him low in the belly. Jubal didn't have time to dodge away, and a club of a fist pounded into his upper arm, staggered him back up against the bar. With a malicious grin crumpling his face, Ogden went for him. But Jubal made a side step, and Ogden thudded full force against the bar. The structure shuddered, and those spectators sitting atop slipped prudently to the floor.

Jubal's shoulder hurt and his fists felt numb and heavy. As Ogden turned back to face him, he set his feet and poled straight up at the mass of black bearded jaw. A crack sounded in the fingers of his hand, and searing pain leaped up his arm. Ogden shook his head and spat blood.

'You gone an' broke my hand, you brainless ox,' Jubal cursed.

'There's more comin',' Ogden put back. 'I sure ain't finished with you yet.'

Jubal backed away. There was something in Ogden's manner that made him realize that this wasn't a chance encounter: it was a set-up. The big man was serving up a planned brawl.

Jubal was momentarily distracted when Ogden caught him in the belly. It wasn't a full weighted blow, but it slammed the air from him and jolted his insides. He fell back into the men who had pressed forward eagerly, felt their hands pushing him forward again. Then the lamps around the saloon started to spin and Ogden became a looming, bulky shape that closed around him. His feet cleared the floor, and he felt the seize of the man's great arms. He yelled with despairing strength, brought his knee up sharply into Ogden's groin.

Ogden grunted and bent forward, but he didn't release his hold on Jubal. He lifted him against his chest, slowly tightened his arms slowly. Jubal smelled his feral body odour, the rancid skin shirt, the sourness of whiskied breath. He squirmed, wrenched his arms and let himself go limp.

As though to lock into a more secure grip, Ogden relaxed his hold. It was the shortest moment that Jubal wanted and he reached out with his left hand. He snatched at one of Ogden's bearded cheeks, drove his right thumb cruelly into his eye.

With a yell of razor-sharp pain, the giant released his hold. Jubal jumped back, sucked breath into his lungs and kicked out as hard as he could.

Ogden had a great, thick-knuckled hand clamped over his right eye. He was roaring, insensible to Jubal and the fight. But Jubal knew that if the injured man recovered enough to get another hold on him, he'd probably die. He swung his boot a second time, and Ogden staggered back. He stepped forward and kicked him a third time in the side of his badly wounded head.

Ogden struck the floor heavily. He rolled on to his back, his chest rising and falling, his breath laboured and grating.

As Jubal stood buckle-kneed, McRae edged close to hand him a glass of whiskey.

'For a moment there, I thought—' Jubal started to say, but the trail boss stopped him.

'I'd have shot him for you,' he said, and smiled. 'Drink this, an' we can all think o' runnin' away.'

Jubal swallowed the fiery liquid and coughed harshly.

The crowd of drinkers and gamblers had been silenced. They broke up self-consciously, as though feeling guilty at having witnessed an ambush fight. But it didn't last, and soon jokes were being made and fresh rounds of drinks were being ordered.

Dummy Parsons was still winded and now bridling with anger. 'Goddamnit, he just caught me off guard,' he railed. 'I could o' taken him . . . given time.'

Yeah, o' course you could, you ol' biscuit roller,' Jubal said with a tired smile. 'If not, Bull here was ready to shoot him dead. Ain't that right, Bull?'

'Yeah. Although you'd probably need a Big Fifty to do it.'

As they turned to leave the saloon, Kingsley Post shouldered his way through the general hubbub. His face was set tight, and he spoke in an incredulous, taken-aback way. 'Someone been handin' out a lesson in good behaviour to one o' my customers?' he said.

'Yeah, somethin' like that. You should try it some time,' Jubal countered.

Post lingered a moment while he lit a fresh cigar. 'You boys have any trouble movin' the herd in?' he asked.

'Our trouble ain't been with cows,' McRae replied sharply. 'What's your interest?'

Post winked at the trail boss. 'Dudley Arnwood's sold out to me.'

McRae and Jubal glanced at each other then back at Post. Unsure of a suitable response, they allowed him to carry on.

'Yeah, he came to see me last night an' made the offer. He looked an' sounded as if he was scared stiff o' somethin''. I just obliged him in the sale. When are you takin' tally?'

'Most likely tomorrow. Some time after noon,' McRae replied unhurriedly.

'Good. I'll have my men there,' Post said. Then he offered a curt good evening and took his leave.

'Well that's somethin' to look forward to,' Jubal said with a painful grimace. 'I'll be there myself, if I can get up into a saddle.' For a moment he stared after Post. Then he walked stiffly from the saloon and his men followed close behind.

Back in the street, Jubal leaned against the hitch rack. 'These sort o' towns should have field hospitals for them who want to leave,' he gritted.

McRae put a hand on his shoulder. 'Worst ones call 'em Boot Hill.'

Jubal turned to Daniel Crane. 'Dan, you an' Erskine get the horses. We'll meet over at the stable.'

As the cousins went off, Jubal glanced back at the saloon, saw Post watching them from a streetside window. There's somethin' I'm missin'. What the hell is it? he wondered and turned back to Dummy Parsons. 'Dummy, we'll be gone inside o' ten minutes. You stay here,' he told him. 'An' say nothin' to nobody.'

Back in the saloon, Post had shoved Bear Ogden into his office. 'I sure got me a Ioser in you,' he started off. 'Goddamn it, what happened?'

'I got half blinded,' Ogden growled back. 'Now you give me what was promised, Mr Post.'

'Take this,' he said and flipped a gold coin on to the top of his desk. 'In the mornin' take it to the doc's an' see what it'll buy you. There'll be more when you do the job properly.'

Ogden glared at him for a long indecisive moment. Then he grunted, lumbered grumpily from the office.

9

The first flash was like the flare of a match. The second held, grew until they heard the deep, distant roar of the blast. Then the light faded in the utter blackness.

Jubal pulled rein. 'Hey, Bull, there's a bird that trails its wing like it's broke,' he said. 'It does it to draw the fox away from its chicks,' he added almost absent-mindedly.

'Yeah, the bobwhite,' Bull McRae answered. 'What you sayin'?'

'I'm sayin' that last night's encounter makes sense. From now on, we got to stay close. If there's any shootin' be damn sure you ain't shootin' friends.'

Jubal nudged his horse forward. He sensed a heavy cloud mass overheard, and he hoped it wouldn't rain. They rode a hard gallop, but soon there was another flash and Jubal made out trees and rocks in the light. A deep explosive rumble caused his horse to swerve, and Jubal tightened his grip on the reins, called out a reassurance. Then he heard the trample of running hoofs, the bawling of panic-stricken cattle, and from several points in the basin, steady bursts of rifle fire.

Then another explosion roared, and in the blossoming glare, he saw the dark rolling wave of cattle, saw them scattering in all directions from the basin. Before the darkness closed again, he caught sight of the two riders.

They men had rifles, and on the far slope of the entrance, were shooting down into the stampeding herd. Jubal saw the chamber flashes and heard the sharp reports as he started to circle wide. Now he could smell the rising dirt and the steers, see their dark rushing shapes, hear their wild bawling as he guided his startled horse. He reined in, then kneed the mount into a quick spurt and swung it round as shadows weaved and plunged around him.

Then his horse stumbled. He pulled against the reins, forced the animal's head up, held it until it regained its footing. He shouted words of comfort, twisted hard right, tight round until they were facing the slope. The shots were behind him now, sharp among the dull rumble of hoofs. They lunged forward, climbed until they were above the stampede. He swung down, tied the reins into a scrub oak and, crouching low, went forward. He ran until he saw the two riders again. Both their horses were fearful and fractious, but the men only had to sit their saddles. They had nothing more to do than point their rifles at the steady stream of cattle and pull triggers.

Jubal moved up on them. If they make a fight, I'll take one of 'em for Billy Boy, he thought. The other one's goin' to tell me who's payin' their fight wages.

Jubal trusted the darkness would add to surprise. 'Hold it right there,' he shouted forcefully. But the men were too wound up to surrender. They twisted in their saddles, and fired blindly. Jubal winced, crouched lower and fired off the shot he'd got planned. He heard the dull thump as the bullet found its mark, saw the nearest rider slump forward when his horse pawed at the sky. The animal snorted violently and Jubal saw it buck again, before charging into the darkness with an empty saddle. Jubal could see where the man fell and, covering the dark form, he ran forward. He kneeled, and with the barrel of his Colt pushed the man's chin out from the body. The man was dead. 'No matter,' he muttered. 'Someone's goin' to know you.'

Jubal remained for a few moments. He decided the second rider had fled, then hurried back to his horse. There was no more gunfire, and the sound of stampeding cattle had ebbed away. He was about to climb into his saddle when he realized he was close to where Dummy Parsons had set the chuck wagon. He walked the horse on, heard the rising, awful noise of steers in pain. Then he cursed vehemently, made a grab for his Colt as Bull McRae rode up.

'They'll be headed for the hills by now,' the trail boss shouted. 'Do you know who they were?'

'I got a fair idea,' Jubal rasped back. 'An' I should've known what they were plannin',' he added desolately.

'Looks like the wagon's wrecked,' McRae said. 'Might as well set fire to it.'

Fifteen minutes later, they had a blaze going. In the spread of its light, they were staring silently at the remnants of Dummy Parsons' cooking when Daniel and Erskine Crane appeared.

'We found Wes,' Daniel told them. 'He got trampled real bad. We only knew it was him 'cause o' them fancy spurs.'

'Don't know where Owen is,' Erskine added. 'We just saw his horse.'

'I'm here, an' I'll live.' With one hand clasping a bleeding shoulder and his face twisted with distress, Owen Chase came stumbling towards the fire. 'Are my boys here?' he gasped. 'Is Ferdie an' Brad, here?'

'No, not here, Owen, but they can't be far,' Jubal said hopefully. Then he turned to Daniel Crane. 'Ride to Pitchfork, Dan, and get a doctor. Use force if you have to, but get him out here. An' have a wagon sent out.'

With Bull McRae tending his wound, Owen Chase told of what had happened. He and Wes Drayton had taken the early watch and, at midnight, he'd checked the remuda before turning in. At the first blast, two riders had fired on him, but he'd managed to crawl away, up the slope. That's where he'd lain, wounded and unconscious until a short while ago. 'Find my boys . . . please find 'em,' he gasped, his voice still trembling with shock.

McRae nodded at Jubal. 'I'll look after him. Maybe they'll turn up,' he said.

Jubal mounted his horse and rode slowly away. All around him now he saw the dark shapes of dead steers. He came across another mangled carcass and the acrid cloy of dynamite was strong. Every few minutes he called out for the Chase boys, but he'd nearly reached the hills before he got an answer.

'Hey, Pa. Is that you, Pa?' the plaintive voice called back.

Bradley Chase sat propped against a boulder. His left leg was stretched awkwardly in front of him, the knee shattered by a rifle bullet.

'It'll soon be daylight, Brad. Your father ain't too bad an' the doc's on his way,' Jubal encouraged.

'Where's Ferdie?' the boy asked.

'I don't know,' Jubal answered truthfully. 'But I found you, didn't I?'

'The boy won't be kickin' up his heels again,' the doctor said, having first taken a look at young Jim. 'I've cleaned an' dressed what I can . . . given 'em both somethin' to ease the pain. I can't do any more until I get 'em to town.'

'Thanks, Doc. We'll go see if we can make 'em a family again,' Jubal replied.

The buzzards came with the dawn, and coyotes were standing off along the edge of the basin. Jubal saw the brush fences had gone, and Frank Pinner, who'd brought the wagon out from Pitchfork, peered at the Copper Hills.

'There's a lot o' cattle scattered across there. We'll be a good many days roundin 'em up,' he said, angrily.

Jubal frowned, 'Who do you suppose was back of the raid, Frank?' he asked. 'Are you sure you didn't recognize that fellow?'

Pinner shook his head. 'Never seen him before. We'll get him onto the wagon. There might be someone in town who knows what his colours are,' he said.

The buzzards were everywhere now. They waddled, heavy-bellied from one carcass to another. Less than fifty yards ahead, two coyotes were snapping and snarling at each other. 'For Chris'sakes, there's enough goddamn beef here to feed the whole o' the Midwest,' Jubal snapped.

As he rode on, Jubal suddenly understood what was happening ahead of him, and he kicked hard with his spurs. The dogs were still rapt in their shocking gorge as he drew down on them. He pulled his Colt and shot one dead; the other one slinked into the brush, still slathering and yelping with fury. Pinner was riding up fast as Jubal was already swinging to the ground.

'What the hell's this?' he started. Then he choked. 'Oh, no.'

'Yeah. Looks like we found Ferdie,' Jubal said quietly.

Ferdinand Chase lay on his back, and half his face and

neck had been chewed away. Jubal turned the body over, groaned when he saw two bullet holes high in the boy's back. He stood up and cursed, fired more bullets into the brush and cursed again.

10

Early one morning, and nearly a week later, Jubal rode from the yard of Hester Box's ranch. The hills were fresh from two days' rain, and a low sun reflected brightly in the road. Since the raid, Jubal and his men had been using the ranch house as their headquarters. This morning, the crew had gone to see how Owen Chase and his son were faring, but Jubal had other things on his mind.

Though nearly everyone in town had had a look at the body of the man Jubal had shot, no one had known his identity. The sheriff had arrived the morning of Billy's funeral, had questioned Jubal about the shooting as if it were a tedious chore rather than his duty. He'd spoken to Owen Chase about the raid, then made a short and unsuccessful attempt to track those responsible.

'Might as well trail a fart,' he'd said. The next morning he took the stage back to Rockford and hadn't been heard from since.

Jubal had looked for Bear Ogden, but had found no trace of him; Snoop Kirkland too had apparently vanished into thin air. Marshal Jeffs had promised to hold either of them, if and when he caught them in town.

*

News of the raid and the killings had roused the folk of Pitchfork. Grumpy men gathered on street corners, some of them giving their arms the first airing since the end of the war. Some strangers were regarded with open, hostile suspicion.

Jubal missed none of this. He understood his ground, realized that many would consider that the trouble had started when he first arrived.

He dismounted outside of Kingsley Post's saloon. At this time of day, there were only three or four customers, and John Tolliver was one of them. He was talking to the bartender, but they stopped, looked up as Jubal entered.

'Is Kirkland around?' Jubal asked them.

Tolliver grinned unpleasantly. 'Ain't you found him yet?' he jibed. 'He must've dug himself a real deep hole.'

Jubal regarded him for a silent moment. 'Just tell me if you've seen him,' he said, at the edge of tolerance.

The bartender took a step sideways closer to Jubal. He was burly man with big forearms, and Jubal decided he wouldn't want to caught by one. The man dropped a hand below the counter, and Jubal reckoned a face full of buckshot might be worse.

'Mister,' the bartender growled, 'I ain't forgot last week. You ain't welcome.'

Jubal thought it was an explicit warning, but he continued. 'I asked you a civil question, Deputy,' he pushed. 'If I have to make it otherwise, I will.'

Tolliver looked at the bartender, and Jubal's eyes flicked suspiciously between them. He hoped his stance was that of a man happy for them to take him on.

The deputy marshal recognized it. He grunted, gave a small compliant smile. 'Most animal life crawls off to lick its wounds when it's hurt,' he suggested drily.

'Where'd that be?'

'In a shack, back o' the lumber yard. You know the place. It's where Ralph Sand used to live.'

Jubal nodded. 'What makes you think I know where that is?' he asked. 'Never mind, I'll find it. Is Post in?'

'No. He's at his ranch.'

Jubal had what he wanted to know. 'Yeah, well, I do know where that is,' he said, and turned on his heel.

A half-hour later, Jubal was telling Hirkam Jeffs that he'd checked out Kirkland's shack.

'Looks like he left in one goddamn hurry,' he put to the town marshal. Then he spoke of his suspicions.

'You think Kingsley Post's the brass nuts?' Jeffs said after listening quietly. 'You're sayin' he paid Bear Ogden to pick a fight with you an' your crew?'

'Yeah, that's exactly what I'm sayin'. Like I was tellin' my trail boss, it's the way a bobwhite draws off the fox. We was meant to be occupied here in town.'

'Don't make sense, a man stampedin' an' killin' his own cattle.'

'He didn't . . . not to his own cattle. His share's safe enough.'

'I still can't see it,' Jeffs grunted. 'Give me one reason why a successful businessman would pull a stunt like that.'

Jubal glanced out the window and sighed. 'To get more successful, might be one,' he muttered, but more to himself than to Jeffs. Then he turned more purposefully to the marshal. 'He wanted a clear field at the basin. He learned we were in town, an' figured he'd give us more to think about than the herd. Incidentally, is he a member o' the town council?' he added.

'Yeah.'

'Did he have anythin' to do with hirin' your deputy?'

Jeffs shrugged. 'He recommended him to the fathers. They'd have had to sweet talk him, though. A town this size, don't pay much.'

'Yeah, must be difficult unless you're drawin' a brace wage from Post.'

Jeffs rubbed his pale, rheumy eyes. 'Wouldn't that be somethin' to prove?' he said, and heaved a sigh.

'Sounds like you might have given it some thought,' Jubal came back drily. 'Then there's Post's crew to consider. They ain't your everyday 'punchers. Where'd he hire 'em?'

'Most of 'em are drifters.'

'Scum, more likely. An' let's not forget the man himself,' Jubal suggested. 'How long's he been here? How'd he get started up?'

'He's one o' the fortunates who rose up from piss alley. That was a couple o' years ago. Since then he's bought out the lumber yard an' moved his saloon to where it is now – the corner o' the main street. Last year he bought the KP ranch.'

Jubal laughed derisively. 'An' you think all that came from sellin' rotgut, do you, Marshal? Huh, I'll bet right now he's got twenty, maybe thirty men on his payroll.'

'He's certainly learned how to turn a fast buck,' Jeffs said, a bit irked. 'Maybe a rich uncle willed him somethin'.'

'Yeah, an' maybe he didn't.' Jubal snorted with disgust and got up. He went to the door and flicked out his cigarette, then he turned back to Jeffs. 'Everythin' that's happened, points to Kingsley Post. Kirkland spread the word when I came into town with Billy, an' only Tolliver knew what we talked about in this office. Unless *you* spread the word, Marshal.'

'You know better'n that,' Jeffs snapped back.

'Yeah. So Tolliver told Sand, and he decided to do somethin' about it at the Hump Rib. Post was there with his henchman, don't forget. It didn't go quite the way it was supposed to, an' Sand got knifed to keep him quiet. For all we know, Snoop Kirkland's gone the same way.'

'You sure put an interestin' slant on things, Lord,' Jeffs said. 'Just bear in mind that Post's got a lot o' support in this town. He's been a benefactor to a lot of its—'

'A lot of it's *who,* Marshal? What are you suggestin'?' Jubal interrupted.

'Goddamnit, feller, I don't know. You got me thinkin' all sorts o' queer stuff,' Jeffs said, with a shake of his head. Then he cleared his throat. 'Do you know about Owen Chase's boy?'

'Bradley? What about him?' Jubal said.

'The doc had to take his leg off, last night. The knee was too smashed up to mend.'

Jubal sighed. 'I ain't too surprised, I saw what was left of it. It's somethin' else that's got to be paid for. You'd like to think I'm barkin' up the wrong tree, wouldn't you?' he asked after a short silence.

'I think the town's gone haywire since you got here,' Jeffs retorted by way of an answer. 'An' I've known Kingsley Post a darn sight longer than I've known you.'

'That's true enough. Then again, you've known yourself a darn sight longer than that. Think on it, marshal.' Jubal said as he walked from the office.

11

'You heard what's happened to Brad?' Owen Chase asked, the moment Jubal entered his room at the Hump Rib. The injured man was in the bed recently occupied by Ase Linder. He sat up, his upper arm and shoulder were swathed in bandages.

Jubal nodded. 'Yeah, the marshal told me. I'm sorry, Owen,' he replied.

Chase stared out through the window up towards the brightening sky. His face was strain tired, sallow and suddenly much older.

'A broken cow prodder with one boy dead an' another crippled for life. Just let Pastor Weems tell me there's a prayer for that,' he rasped bitterly. 'You brought the money? You want to buy me out?' he asked.

'No, Owen. You'll be back there before long.'

'I never want to see the place again.' Chase paused. 'It belonged to the boys. That's how I thought of it,' he said. 'What's the point?'

'Right now there ain't one,' Jubal accepted. 'But there might be tomorrow, or the day after. You got to wait an' see.'

'So where are you goin' to settle? If you are goin' to.'

'Dunno. The last few days, I guess I been feelin' a bit like you.'

'Why not run your beef with mine?' Chase then suggested. 'Maybe we can work somethin' out after the fall roundup. If you don't I'll probably sell to Post.'

Jubal's face darkened. 'Has he made you an offer?' he asked.

'No, not yet. But he will. An' it'll be while I'm still stuck up here.'

Jubal gave Chase's offer a second thought. He'd hardly enough cattle to warrant leasing Adam's Stamp from Essie Linder, and not nearly enough to keep Bull McRae and Erskine Crane on any sort of payroll. Daniel had gone to work for Hester Box, but he would like to keep the other two men with him.

'All right, Owen, we'll try it an' see how it works out,' he decided. He got up, gently touched the man's hand. 'When you're out o' here, we'll talk it over proper.'

'I'm not goin' back, Jube,' he said gravely. 'Nothin's goin' to change that.'

Jubal smiled sympathetically. 'Then give some thought to what you are goin' to do when you're up an' out o' this bed.'

'Oh, I already have,' Chase confirmed, and for the shortest moment, his whole being froze. 'I'm goin' to find who's responsible, an' when I do, I'll kill him. Do you understand that?'

'Yeah, I understand,' Jubal answered sincerely. 'Me an' you got a lot in common.'

Jubal ate a hurried meal in the hotel's small dining-room. If his suspicions held water, he thought he knew where Kirkland would be holed up. The only way to find out was by riding to the KP ranch.

*

Kingsley Post sat in his ranch-house office and wondered if he'd gone too far. The valley was in an uproar over what had befallen the Chase family. There were some folk of town standing who were beginning to push for action. If a federal issue was made of the trouble, and if they talked to Jubal Lorde and learned about Snoop Kirkland, things could turn out to be very difficult.

Post was very fortunate that the man whom Jubal Lorde had killed, hadn't been recognized as an employee of his. He took a deep, shaky breath and looked out at the men who sat around the corral. They were swapping small talk, and Kirkland was one of them. He was the one who worried Post. The manner in which he windmilled his arms and stabbed the air around him, gave the impression of someone with a runaway mouth. Post didn't like it, and he raised the window.

'Kirkland,' he shouted. 'Can you give me a minute?'

'You want me, boss?' Grif Benton asked.

'No, but stick around.'

Post was going to tell Kirkland to take a seat but changed his mind. He took a fat envelope from his desk drawer and counted out $200.

'I want you out o' the country,' he said, and tossed the money towards Kirkland. 'Head for Montana, an' let me know when you get there. Then keep quiet and stay until you hear otherwise.'

Kirkland looked at the money and grimaced. 'Stay?' he echoed. 'You make me sound like some sort o' heeler dog, Mr Post.' Gobbets of white spittle appeared at the corners of his mouth when he saw the tight smile of Post's response. He contemplated the money for a long moment before his mouth opened again. 'Sure,' he grunted. 'I'll take me a hotel room somewhere. But I'll likely be needin' a sight more'n this,' he added, picking up the bills and shoving them into his pocket. 'Let's hope I don't have to try elsewhere when I run dry.'

'I said you'll hear from me. An' don't go anywhere near Pitchfork,' Post concluded icily, as Kirkland backed unsteadily from the room.

Post ground his teeth, seethed at Kirkland's implied threat. There was no doubting what the man meant. He knew that if given a chance, Kirkland would blackmail him.

He waited until Kirkland had ridden away, then he called Benton. His man listened, then nodded briefly as he understood. A moment later he saddled up, and Post watched as he rode off through the home pasture.

Essie May Linder was lying on the rim of the grassy rise that overlooked the KP ranch. But she only let her eyes follow Grif Benton briefly before she shifted her attention back to the ranch house. She had been there a full hour, waiting to get a shot at Kingsley Post.

The sun moved slowly leaving the porch in the shadow of the two-storey house. Spread around the hard-pummelled dirt of the broad yard, there were four outhouses and a long bunkhouse. Along the top rail of one corral, saddles glinted in the sunlight, and a handful of men hunkered below them. They'll be waiting for the day's orders, Essie thought.

She knew Post was in the house because she'd already spotted his big grey mare. She put her rifle down for a moment and rubbed her brows with the tips of her fingers. Then, as she shifted her position, the front door opened.

But the porch was in deep shadow now, and she couldn't see him clearly. She rested her elbows on the ground, took a deep breath and brought the front and back sights into line. She pressed her cheek against the stock as he moved into the bead she'd drawn. He was on the top porch and he stopped moving to fumble for something in his pocket. Essie's arms stiffened, she exhaled slowly, and her finger felt gently for the trigger. Then, as she was about to squeeze, she heard the dull sound of nearby hoofs.

She cursed and flicked a sidelong glance across her shoulder. But the tension of the movement tightened her hand, and the rifle crashed out across the rangeland.

Her taut nerves snapped, and she watched mesmerized as startled yells spread across the yard. She saw Post running from the porch, men running to the bunkhouse for their rifles. Two of them fired off their Colts, but they were too far away to be effective. Essie gulped, worked her way backwards down the slope.

Well below the rim of the rise, Jubal Lorde was vigilantly sitting his own mount. 'Where's your horse?' he called out, as Essie broke into a run.

'At the valley road,' she uttered, the words nearly choking as she looked up and pointed.

'They'll soon be crawlin' over this ridge like flies. If I was you, I'd start runnin'. Get out o' here,' Jubal said, his voice gritted with command.

Essie nodded, watched anxiously as Jubal pulled his rifle from the saddle holster and heeled his mount away from the ridge, towards the tree-line. Her heart pounded as she ran on to the bottom of the slope.

A moment longer and she would have put a bullet into Kingsley Post. But now Jubal Lorde was paying the price of her failure. He would probably lead Post and his riders east, while she made her escape west, back towards her Rod 4 ranch. It reminded her of a school picture book, where a prairie rooster feigned a broken wing to lead a predator away from its chicks.

12

Jubal broke from the trees and reined in. A long, rolling meadow lay before him, and it was dotted with grazing cattle. There's too many . . . too many in one spot, he thought. It was either a spring gather, or Post was getting ready to drive them into higher country.

He patted his horse's warm neck, looked to where he could see the weather vane atop Post's ranch house. He knew he'd been spotted and he sat his horse, waited for the riders to show, so's to lead them off. He looked beyond the meadow, beyond the rolling hills to where gnarled pine began its sharper climb to the Wind River timberline.

Then he saw two riders had galloped into sight. Then four more were galloping towards him, and he walked his horse forward a few steps. A small puff of smoke blossomed alongside the nearest horseman and a bullet whined close. The flat crack of the shot rang out, and he knew that was them. There'd been five men at the corral and Post would be the sixth, on his big grey.

Two more shots carried on the breeze, and Jubal swung his horse broadside. 'Too close,' he muttered and pulled his rifle. 'Be goddamn lucky to hit anythin' from here, but if you keep still . . .' he said, and levelled the gun. He picked the nearest rider and squeezed the trigger. 'I might get lucky next time,' he shouted, and turned his horse towards the cattle. Most of them had lifted their heads at the shots, now they scattered, started their mindless run at his approach. But riding through the herd gave Jubal a brief period of refuge. To close in on him, the chasing riders would have to swerve and dodge the treacherous horns of the running steers.

The terrain lifted a little, and the twisted pines were now less than a quarter-mile ahead. It looked like if he could gain them, he'd find good cover, and Jubal spurred his tired horse. He couldn't keep going at this rate, and those chasing him were mounted on fresh horses. He cursed aloud, slid his rifle back into the boot, and galloped straight into trouble.

Two of the chasing riders had swung away from the cattle that Jubal had hoped to put between them, and now they were closing in on him from their right flank. One of them hauled in his mount and took a quick shot. Jubal pulled his own Colt, but his horse suddenly jumped in midstride. It snorted furiously as the bullet creased his shoulder, split its hide in a red, ragged line.

The two riders steadied their mounts to try again. For Jubal, there was no way to avoid them except to turn back, and the others were closing in on him. He aimed the best he could and fired at the nearest man. The rider's horse reared back on its hind legs and pawed at the sky. Jubal fired again, and this time the stricken animal fell on its side and took the rider down with it.

The second man was less than twenty feet away when he fired. Jubal felt his horse falter as the bullet found its mark. The man fired again, and Jubal's left leg jolted from the impact. It felt as though a branding iron was being driven into his thigh.

He rolled from the saddle, once again drew the rifle from its boot, and stumbled towards the cover of a stunt pine. It was a bad spot to be in. When the men following got to shouting distance, all of them could work together. They'd have him trapped. He wanted to make an attempt at the trail that led on and up to the timberline, but his leg was spearing agonizing flames into his hip. He took a laboured breath and limped forward.

He made it about a quarter of the way up the long incline, and the tops of the pine were almost level with him now. He could hear the horses closing, and an occasional shout from the riders. Some of them had taken a longer ride to get above him, and some dust and dirt spilled down. He cursed and his heart hammered against his ribs when he realized they were almost upon him.

He wondered if, at that moment, Essie was safe at her ranch. At least her standpoint had been made clear. She might be in cahoots with Post, but there was a hopeful bit, in that she also wanted to kill him. Must be an advantage there, he thought grimly.

Then he wondered where Post was – if he'd gone back to scout the ridge.

From somewhere out among the trees, he heard a long shout, and one of the riders above him yelled back a response.

Jubal knew he couldn't be seen from above, so he straightened himself and moved forward, stopped in his tracks as the horsemen came in single file down through the pine.

'We've gone an' found each other,' he muttered, and brought the rifle up to chest height. 'Hold up, fellers,' he rasped out. 'My hands are shakin' so bad, I might just shoot the wrong 'un. Unbuckle your gunbelts, then drag out your rifles an' drop them too. Make a sound, an' you're dead.'

When the men had discarded their guns, Jubal ordered them to turn their horses back the way they had come. 'An' start walkin',' he added sharply.

As they started to move off, another voice called out. 'Hey there, Marley, we got Lorde's horse. He couldn't have got far. He must be somewhere near you.'

'We're here, Ike,' one of Jubal's captives returned quickly. 'Yeah, he's real near us. He's got a big gun barrel stuck up my ass. So you be careful when you take him.'

Anger immediately tore through Jubal. 'I told you,' he hissed. The horse shielded most of the man, so Jubal fired down at his feet. The horse lunged forward almost trampling the man, but he stumbled to his knees, then rolled on to his side.

'You nearly shot my goddamn toes off,' he yelled groping at his bloodied boot.

'Then you'd have been hoppin' all the goddamn way home,' Jubal snarled back.

Jubal mounted one of the horses, and made the pair of them hang on to a stirrup of the other one. After ten minutes, when pursuit didn't show itself, Jubal thought that maybe they would be first to reach the basin rim. The two men were labouring, their clothing was black with sweat and their mouths were cake dry. The man with the shattered foot fell to his knees, bent forward unable to rise.

'You might not have thought of it, but you two bozos are in some sort o' race. The loser gets his *whole* foot shot off,' Jubal threatened him.

But Jubal's own pain was dulling him, and he'd lost a lot

of blood. If he moved around too much, the bullet might find itself a nice thick vein to squeeze. If his leg didn't get some doctoring, he doubted he'd last long enough to get the truth out of Essie.

The three men had almost gained the rim of the basin, but both Post's men were on the point of collapse. Jubal wasn't going to let them ride, he wanted them dead on their feet. Eventually the first man crawled ahead to make the boulder-strewn rim, the horse followed, its muscles bunching under its sweaty hide. The next man with his bloody foot, lay collapsed. His breath was rattling in his throat and he was totally exhausted.

'I ain't goin' any further. Shoot me if you want,' he gasped and closed his eyes.

Jubal drew his Colt to get the man up and moving, when he heard the sounds to his left. But there was nothing to see, and it was the voice to his right that got to him. 'Drop the Colt, Lorde. Drop it or die. Make your choice,' the man directed.

13

After riding from his ranch with the crew, Kingsley Post rode to Pitchfork. When he was beyond Hester Box's ranch, he met with Grif Benton. His henchman's quiet confidence pleased Post. Men like Benton were rare in that their goal wasn't beyond their ability to achieve it.

'Business taken care of,' Benton said.

'Good. Did anyone see you?' Post wanted to know.

'No. We was above Messenger's place. He was diggin' taters or some such, an' would've heard the shot, though. Right about now, an' good citizen that I'm sure he is, he's bringin' Kirkwood to town across the back of his plough mare.'

As they approached town, Post told Benton what had happened at the ranch.

His henchman looked doubtful. 'How sure are you it was Lorde who fired that shot?' he asked.

'I told you, we spotted him.'

'That ain't the same thing,' Benton suggested. 'He misses his shot, then pops up like a sittin' duck? You got to admit that's pretty dumb.'

'Well, that's what happened. There was enough goddamn witnesses,' Post insisted.

They were at the outskirts of town when they learned that Toby Messenger had already arrived with Kirkland's body. Further on, an angry knot of men were already gathered out front of the marshal's office. Members of the town council were grim and indignant at the evidence of another violent death in their once peaceful community.

It didn't take Post long to decide that he had himself a store-bought situation. By playing his cards right, he could fork all the blame on to Jubal Lorde. At the same time, he'd be reinforcing his own position as local benefactor and upholder of the law.

He waved to Fergus Tapping who owned the corn merchants and general mercantile. 'Hey, Fergus, I've got an idea on how to end all this,' he called out. 'Get some folk over to the KP in ten minutes, an' I'll explain. Tell Jeffs an' Tolliver, there's drinks on the house.'

A quarter-hour later, Post was pouring shots of his cheap whiskey for those who were gathered excitedly around him.

'I heard what some o' you were sayin', but we don't want to send for the militia just yet. It won't do the reputation o' the town any good, an' it could kill off business for years ahead. No, we'll go for handlin' this trouble ourselves,' he said commandingly.

There was some all round sipping of the house drinks, then concerned mumbling turned to tentative accord.

'I'm suggestin' that our own legally appointed officer of the law, John Tolliver, takes a posse out to arrest Lorde an' whoever's on his payroll,' he continued. 'Blood's spilled too far over, an' it must be stopped.'

Post called for the barman to open up another bottle and he smiled inwardly at the success of his provocation. 'Since I have the men, an' let's not pretend otherwise, *the inclination*,' he said with an enigmatic smile, 'I'll bear the cost and responsibility. All our futures are at stake here, gentlemen. So let's do somethin' about it.'

There was now a wound-up murmur of voices. Post had won them over, despite the silent disapproval of Marshal Jeffs. It was agreed that John Tolliver should lead a posse to arrest Jubal Lorde, and there was to be no violence. Those under arrest were to be taken to Faithful Jail where they would await trial.

Ten minutes later, Post stood beside Hirkam Jeffs on the boardwalk. 'Well, you managed to keep your feelin's in the fraidy hole, Marshal. What *do* you think?' he asked.

Jeffs lifted his hand close to Post's face, made a little gap between his thumb and forefinger. 'I think you were this much from takin' the law into your own hands. Don't ever do it again,' he warned.

Post nodded. 'Won't have to. That was the point,' he said seriously. Then he chuckled. 'Don't worry, Hirk. Your job's about to get a whole lot easier.'

But there was still one person who could create a stumbling block for Post's objective. And that was Esther May Linder. She already knew too much about him, and now he wondered what would happen when she heard about the meeting in his saloon, He reckoned she had to hear about it from him. And hear it sooner rather than later. Much sooner.

Hester Box stood on her porch and faced Toby Messenger. Messenger had been in town during the meeting, but he'd stood just outside the corner door of the saloon. He'd remained more or less out of sight, had heard the results of the meeting when a few men had pushed out into the street. He had ridden at once to tell Hester.

'An' you believe all this, Toby?' she asked him, disbelievingly. 'You believe Jubal Lorde killed Billy? What else is there?'

Messenger drew the edge of a cracked boot through the porch dust. His freckled face was full of uncertainty. 'I don't know what else. I don't know what to think, Essie,' he said. 'All I know is, you an' me were gettin' along fine until he arrived. Then you changed.'

'No Toby. You're the one who's changed,' she said impatiently. 'You've got yourself stirred up about somethin' that just isn't true. I'm not your toy that's been confiscated.'

'I've seen you with him,' he said bitterly. 'You can't see him for what he is. I've a mind to join up with that posse to hunt him down.'

'Yeah, that's the way to let me see you've grown up,' Essie said with an exasperated shake of her head.

Messenger stalked off to collect his horse from the meadow. Hester waited for him to ride off, then she hurried inside to change her dress. She had to warn Frank Pinner and the others about the Kingsley Post riders, and a few minutes later she had her horse galloping towards the Owen Chase spread.

14

There were two of them and they came from the trees, leading their horses. One gripped a rifle at his hip, the other man levelled a long-barrelled Colt at Jubal.

Jubal smiled with cold despair. He considered the option of dying right away or living a while longer, and dropped his Colt. Then he clasped his hands around the pommel, cursed and waited for an outcome.

'Kill the son-of-a-bitch, Ike,' the man who had crawled up ahead to the lip of the rim, yelled out. His face was glazed with sweat and his chest heaved. 'Throw me a gun,' he said, struggling to his feet, stumbling back towards Jubal. 'Give me your gun, goddamnit, Ike. Give me your gun.'

'Here,' the man called Ike said, and tossed a Colt. But the man slipped and bungled the catch.

Jubal looked across to the boulders, fifty, sixty feet away on his right. He thought for an instant he'd seen movement near a stunt pine. He gripped his hands tighter, as in front of him the man reached down and picked up the dropped Colt. The man took a deep breath and straightened, his eyes ablaze with hatred.

'You son-of-a-bitch,' he ranted hoarsely.

'Yeah, you already said,' Jubal snorted back intensely.

As the man pulled back the hammer, there was a shot. Jubal was instantly aware of two things. The shot had come from where he thought he'd seen movement, and the man who was about to shoot him groaned and bent double, grabbed at his elbow.

The man who was covering with a rifle, swung to confront the gunfire. But the hidden marksman fired again, then again, and the man whirled his horse away.

Jubal watched as the men dismounted, as they moved closer together. One was bent over gripping his arm with bloody fingers, the other two were looking left and right, struggling with bridle reins to hold their horses steady.

He reached back, and pulled his rifle from the boot. As he turned with it, Pug Marley got to his feet and shuffled over painfully to join the others. As Jubal looked them over, he felt weak, woozy enough to see their figures becoming blurred. But he saw that the man who'd carried the rifle still had a handgun at his waist.

'You noticed I got me some help,' Jubal said. 'Best get rid of all your hardware.'

The man unbuckled his belt and dropped it to the ground.

'Now all o' you, start walkin' back to the rat's nest you came out of,' Jubal directed tersely.

The four started off towards the relative safety of the trees. Before they got there, Marley, whom Jubal had shot in the foot, turned around.

'You'll be hearin' from me, Lorde,' he shouted. 'I'm makin' it my work to see you dead.'

'Then tell Kingsley Post you want a big pay rise,' he rasped and fired a parting shot just above their heads.

As the echo reverberated across the basin, the men

shuffled off, incensed and disgruntled. Jubal followed until they were well out of sight, then he fired off another two shots. But when he turned back, everything ahead of him started to shimmer, as if he was looking through a waterfall. He bent forward, then tipped sideways from the saddle. He came to momentarily as he hit the ground, long enough to mumble, 'You can come out now,' before the world turned deep blurry black.

This was how Essie found him, lying on his back, his face drawn and blood-drained. She glanced down at his bloodied pants as she lifted his head.

He looked at her with tired, dull eyes. 'I had the strangest dream,' he started to say. 'There was a gang o' men tryin' to kill me. I got half my leg shot off, then trees an' rocks opened fire.'

'You'll have to stop chewin' that locoweed,' Essie said with a small smile.

Jubal rolled on to his side, then eased himself on to his elbow. 'You didn't get the hell out o' here, then?' he said.

'No. This is mostly my fault. Shadowin' you seemed the least I could do. You sent them fellers packin', but you've got a bad wound in the top o' your leg,' she explained. 'I've got some tidyin' up to do, then we can both get away from here.'

Jubal sat himself up, shook his head to clear the fug of weakness and pain. He watched Essie gather up all the guns and gunbelts, and heel them into a patch of scrub. She shoved Jubal's gun under her belt, and carried his rifle back to his horse. She looked at him, saw his hat was gone and his long dark hair hung limp across his forehead.

She shoved the rifle back into the boot and handed him

his Colt. 'If I give you a hand, can you climb back into your saddle?' she asked.

'I'd say yes, even if I couldn't,' he answered with a grim smile.

When Jubal was in the saddle, Essie went to her own horse, then rounded up the other three. She slapped them off towards the valley road. It was in the opposite direction to Post's men, but she thought they'd eventually make it back to their home pasture.

From there on, she rode close to Jubal, stretching out an occasional hand to reassure and steady him, He was rolling, wilting with exhaustion and she knew it was from loss of blood.

'Someone's got to take that bullet from your leg,' she said.

'You done much sawbonin'?' Jubal asked after a long moment's reflection.

'I once squeezed a pea from my brother's nose. How different can it be?'

At walking pace they followed the rising rim of the basin. At the top was a mile-long corridor of boulders that the trail serpentined through. It fell steeply at first then gently as the valley widened.

Essie measured distances in her mind against Jubal's need for immediate attention. The fearful thought struck her that it was ten miles or more to the ranch house, and any one of Post's men could spot them on the way there. She was considering the risk when she realized they couldn't be too far from one of the Rod 4 line shacks. In less than two weeks, the 'punchers would be driving the herds here for summer graze. All the line cabins would have been checked, well stocked for the men who would spend most of the following months up here in the high country.

The trail flattened out as it crossed the valley floor, then lifted again into a wide belt of timber. Beyond the trees, they rode into a long sloping meadow, where tall grass bent and shimmered with the wind. They reined in between tight stands of cedar. Nestled between them was a small log cabin, a lean-to shed and corral.

Essie dismounted and reached up to help Jubal. 'I hope you're carryin' a pocket knife,' she said, and smiled warmly. 'Otherwise it might hurt a bit.'

'No more'n it does at the moment. Believe me,' he answered and returned the smile.

15

Having helped Jubal on to one of the bunks, Essie looked around the small cabin. There was one window, and a bunk either side of a Dutch oven. A rack of open shelves contained canned foods and a few pots, and a skillet hung from a big iron nail. The coffee pot was standing on the hard-packed dirt floor.

She went out and led the horses to the shed, brought in the rifles, and leaned them inside the door. Then she gathered an armload of wood and dumped it in the box next to the stove. She started a fire under the stove, and while waiting for it to take, she walked down to Black Sage Creek. She scoured a wood bucket with a handful of gritty sand, then rinsed it carefully before filling.

When the fire was hot she filled the coffee pot and set a pan of water to boil. Then she lit the central hanging lamp and had a close look Jubal's leg.

'I got to do some tailorin' to your pants,' she said. 'Your knife please.'

She took the small clasp knife and cut Jubal's pants from his hip down to his knee, then both ways across. She gritted her teeth at the exposed wound, the black, bulging rose of flesh. From the wound to his boot, his pants were dark and sticky from the ooze of blood.

'Sorry,' she said, as she pulled the boot off. Jubal let out a low groan, and Essie grimaced at the sight and smell of the blood-soaked stocking.

She tested the water from the stove, then had a quick, futile search for some bandage material. 'No,' she muttered, at the same time, unbuttoning her blouse. She cut through one of the button holes, tore a section from all around the bottom, and put it back on.

She dipped the material in the hot water and gently washed the raw flesh. He groaned and pushed at her with his hand, opened his eyes and raised himself up. He looked enquiringly, blinked and looked around the cabin.

'Hell of a place to die,' he said.

'You got a bullet in your leg. If you do die, it ain't goin' to be here,' she answered calmly.

For the first time, Jubal looked down at his leg. 'Can you see the bullet?' he asked.

'Yeah. You're lucky it's along the top o' your leg. The bullet's gone more across, instead o' down. It ain't too deep, but it's goin' to hurt some.'

She cleaned the knife blade, then unbuckled his belt and drew it through the loops of his pants. 'No, you ain't got lucky, soldier. It's for you to bite on,' she said, and placed it in his hand. 'Whenever you're ready.'

He gave a worried smile then gripped the leather between his teeth. 'Go on, do it,' he mumbled incoherently.

Essie took a breath, and squeezed the lump hard. Jubal's body tensed with pain, and cords of muscle bulged in his jaws and neck. She made a fast, short stabbing motion; an inch long cut, from which bright blood, instantly oozed. Then she forced the point of the blade under the bullet, and pinched the sides of the cut, tight. The bullet popped out, fell from his leg on to the edge of the bunk, then on to the floor.

'Some pea,' she said and kneeled with relief. 'But it didn't hurt as much as I thought it would.'

Sweat now beaded Jubal's face. He took the belt from his mouth, blinked twice to focus on the deep imprint of his teeth. 'I reckon that ol' steer might have felt somethin',' he joked.

'If you've got any tobacco, it works on the healin'. Some sort of antiseptic, apparently,' she offered.

'We ain't wastin' my tobacco on a bullet wound,' Jubal replied. 'If the bullet's out, an' the wounds clean, I'll live. Thanks to you, Essie. Thank you.'

'I'll pour us some coffee,' she said, but Jubal was already falling asleep. 'That's what a wounded deer does,' she muttered. 'Wakes up when it's mended.'

She used another strip of her blouse to cover the wound, then she cut off a large strip of bed blanket to use as top bandage.

Standing outside in the failing light of first dark, Essie thought of the ranch, hoped that Kingsley Post hadn't ridden by and found her gone, She went back to check the stove had enough fuel for a few more hours, and to snuff the lamp. 'I'll be back,' she said. 'There must be some guardian angel in me.'

Jubal lay very still and opened his eyes very slowly. A low, ambient light came from the stove grate, and he could hear the small crackling sounds of the dying fire. 'Hell,' he cursed, and the cabin closed in on him again.

A half-hour Iater, he tentatively swung his legs from the bunk, trod on his belt and cursed. He reached for his Colt, reloaded with awkward fingers as recent events weaved through his slurred mind. He recalled what he was up against, and didn't want to be trapped inside the four walls of the cabin. 'Only got a goddamn leg wound,' he rasped.

He picked up two blankets and his boots, but put them down again as the aroma of coffee cut through the drift of other smells. The coffee had thickened, but he managed one hot, full cup. Marginally picked up, he carried the gear to the shed and bedded down on the floor. But fatigue, and the keen bite of pain still subdued him. Within minutes he was asleep again.

He wasn't aware of how long he slept second time around, only that he awoke with the creepy feeling that he wasn't alone. He stretched out his hand for his Colt, and his heart thumped when he felt the press of a boot across the top of his hand. He lifted his eyes, whispered a tired curse at the hulking figure crouched over him.

'Take it easy,' Bear Ogden grunted from deep in his throat. 'If I'd wanted to hurt you, I'd have done it before now.'

16

The sky was pitted with bright stars when Essie rode wearily across the yard of the Rod 4. Felix Batchelor, the ranch foreman, was pacing anxiously on the veranda. He greeted her with the upset that comes with worry.

'Where you been, Miss Linder? I was goin' to bring the boys out if you weren't back soon,' he said.

'I have stayed out late before, Batch. What's goin' on?' Essie asked, sensing something wasn't right.

'There's talk that Jubal Lorde pulled the raid that got the Chase boy killed. Add that to the jabber about Kirkland, an' the Billy Box shootin', an' the man ain't got much of a future.'

'What?'

'Aye, that's right. Kingsley Post went an' called a town council meetin', an' they voted to have Tolliver lead a posse,' Batchelor said. 'They already got the trail boss, Bull McRae, an' two others in jail. Now they're goin' for Lorde.'

'What are they charged with . . . McRae an' the others?'

Batchelor shrugged. 'No idea, but that's where they are, all right. I hear they sent for the sheriff, again. You best stick close to home until this is settled miss. Lorde's already tried to kill Post, an' he's just as liable to take a shot at any of us here.'

Essie's shoulders slumped despondently. So this is what we've come to, she thought. People with unexciting lives believing rumours because they need to. 'You said so yourself, Batch, it's no more than jibber-jabber.' Just then, Batchelor's wife who was the ranch housekeeper came outside and bustled across the veranda.

'Kingsley Post was here lookin' for you, Essie,' she said. 'He came twice, asked where you was, what you was doin'. I told him, whatever it was, it was your business. Are you ready to eat somethin'?'

'Yes, thank you, Alice,' Essie said and smiled. 'Batch, saddle me a fresh horse, will you?'

'Are you goin' out again . . . before you've ate?' Batchelor asked huffily.

'No,' Essie returned smartly and followed a tetchy looking Alice inside. 'I got to wash up a bit,' she said, when she saw Alice looking at her dirty hands.

'Did he tell you they got a posse up?' Alice asked when they were inside.

'Yes, he told me. He said they've arrested Jubal Lorde's crew.'

'Are you goin' to say where you've been, Essie?' Alice enquired.

'I've been with Jubal Lorde. He's wounded. I didn't tell Batch . . . or anyone.'

'Well, the worst *he* could do, would be to talk you out o' whatever it is you got in mind,' Alice said. 'You know those riders are goin' to be combin' the entire basin tomorrow. Probably beyond.'

Essie ate hungrily, but thoughtfully. She was thinking about moving Jubal, but where would be safe enough.

'If you're ridin' over to see Hester, you'd best shout afore you get there,' Alice advised. 'Batch say there's some eyes out watchin' the place.'

Essie wiped her mouth carefully, looked up after a moment. 'They're not watchin' here are they, Alice?'

'Batch reckons not. Are you goin' to bring him in here?' she asked about Jubal. 'For the time bein' you can put him in your pa's room. Where's he hurt?'

'His thigh. I took the bullet out.'

'Good. The boys will be asleep by the time you get back, So there's no need to go slinkin' round back, an' they'll all be goin' out early mornin'. By the way, I never liked Kingsley Post,' Alice continued. 'I just thought you'd like to know.'

Jubal pulled his hand from under Bear Ogden's foot. 'How long have you been here?' he asked.

Ogden gave a rough chuckle. 'A while. I've been up in the hills. I heard shots an' saw you takin' Post's boys out o' the valley,' he said. 'You sure know how to make friends.'

'Was that you hidin' up?'

'Yeah, I guess. Didn't know you'd seen me.'

'At that moment, I was particularly sensitive to what was goin' on around me.'

Ogden squatted on his heels. 'I ain't ever run away from much before.'

'You ran off 'cause I whupped you?'

'No, it was Post . . . what he wanted me to do for twenty dollars.'

'Huh, I knew it. He paid *you* to whup *me*, didn't he?'

'Yeah, a real *good* whuppin' if you know what I mean.'

'So what are you doin' here, tellin' me all this?' Jubal asked after a moment or two.

'I don't like the way things are pannin' out. I done some stuff; you know . . . with Sand an' Kirkland. God help me.

'Like what?'

'Short stuff. Rustlin' a few head from neighbours. The Bar T, a few o' Chase's, a few from the Box spread.'

'So what's changed? Bring me up to date,' Jubal said.

'I'd like to live a little longer. Post's been pushin' knives into people ever since he got to Pitchfork. With what I know, it's got to be close to my time.'

Jubal nodded understandingly. 'I want to know who the bushwhacker is,' he said directly.

'Well I wouldn't swear to it, but I'd put a bottle o' good stuff on it bein' Ralph Sand. He could use a rifle, an' he was sneakier than a coyote.'

'Was there any stock rustled while Billy Box was in Colorado?'

'No,' Ogden affirmed. 'There must've been some reason . . . somethin' goin' on.'

'Yeah, you ain't kiddin''. An' for one reason or another, Post delayed his raid for one night.'

'Yeah, he did. But you ain't goin' to prove it, or who was there. Those hired hands of his know better'n to talk. Some of 'em are too feared, an' others just don't.'

Jubal sniffed, had another moment's thought. 'Do you want to work for me, Bear?' he asked.

'You'd give *me* a job?'

'Well, I owe you. What's the rate for eye-gougin' a feller? But remember, Post's probably out lookin' for me right now.'

'I ain't got a range o' skills. What would I be doin'?' Ogden rumbled.

'We'll think o' somethin''. Go an' see Hester Box and

Frank Pinner. Tell 'em I'm all right. Tell 'em I said to put you on my payroll. Then find out what's goin' on.'

'OK.' The giant grinned, showed a set of wrecked canines. 'You want me to tell 'em where you are?'

'No, don't do that. They'd come lookin' an' run right into the Post bunch. That would be one hell of a meetin'.'

'OK. Do you know much about Essie Linder?' Ogden then wanted to know.

'Yeah, some. We've had our moments,' Jubal said impassively.

'Well, I hope you ain't down to trustin' her. She's pretty thick with Post. Makes you wonder if she knows as much as I do.'

'There's goin' to be a price paid, 'cause o' what people know about you, Post,' Jubal called out, after Ogden had gone. 'Seems like the value o' your demise is growin' by the hour.'

Within minutes, Jubal's pulse was racing. 'All the goddamn excitement,' he mumbled. He knew that Ogden wasn't a natural liar, that for the most part, what he'd said was true. Now he felt a creeping resentment at the thought that Essie Linder was double-dealing. If she was running with Post, why did she want to kill him? Jubal suddenly felt tired again and he closed his eyes, let it creep over him. What part of the story held the truth about Essie? What was she keeping quiet about when friends and neighbours were being murdered?

In his room at the Hump Rib, Owen Chase sat wedged in his pillows. A little earlier, from the boardwalk below, he'd overheard a group of folk giving their opinion on John Tolliver's posse.

'Goddamn Jubal Lorde,' he seethed. 'It was him all the

time. Him that pulled the raid, him that got my Ferdie shot.'

The man's heart thumped heavily. He pushed his supper tray aside, rolled to the side of the bed, and drew his gunbelt from the bedside cabinet. Trembling with angry emotion, he pulled the sheet back over him, curled his fingers around the butt of his old Colt.

'Come visit me again, why don't you,' he whispered icily.

17

Jubal blinked and looked up at the curtains, then through the window at the sunny sky beyond. He had a vague memory of somewhere else, but it seemed like a long, dark time ago.

'Where's this?' he said suspiciously. 'Where am I?'

Alice Batchelor smiled at him. 'This is Essie May's room,' she replied.

'Essie May? How the hell did I get here?'

'She brought you. An' that's enough blasphemin' if you want to stay,' she reprimanded sternly. 'You had a fever fit to blow a seam.'

'What time is it?'

'Time for you to rest up some more. There's soup an' cold cuts here, so try an' get some of it down. Not too much though, or you'll be sick.'

'Where is Essie?'

'Heaven above knows. She rode out . . . *again.* You know there's a posse out lookin' for you?' she asked.

'Kingsley Post's men?'

'Yes, perhaps I should've said necktie party. There's a lot happened you got to learn about, Jubal Lorde. Don't see why it shouldn't be me, tellin' you.'

For a couple of minutes, Alice told Jubal about Snoop Kirkland's murder, the meeting in town, and the subsequent arrest of Bull McRae and Daniel and Erskine Crane. 'That John Tolliver is leading 'em. If it wasn't for Essie, your hide would be tent-pegged on a hillside.'

'Yeah, I know. The girl's a jewel.' Juba! grimaced and raised himself on to an elbow. 'So, what is it between Essie and Post?'

Alice pondered a moment, then she gave Jubal a shrewd look. 'I don't know what it'll mean to you, but I ain't breakin' any trust if I tell you he wanted a partnership with her, an' I ain't just talkin' business. Huh, he knows Mr Ase ain't goin' to last much longer, an' probably figures it's a means to get his hands on the ranch. O' course it'll be over my dead body.'

Jubal tried a weak smile. 'I'm sure it won't come to that,' he said, and he lay back, took a few moments to think while Alice pottered about the room. There was only one person who knew the truth of his own innocence, and that was Essie. As far as Jubal was concerned, Essie was indeed fundamental to his present and future predicament.

'Where'd you say she was?' he asked.

'I didn't, young man. But she must have had some good reason not to tell me,' Alice admitted. 'Meantime, you stay here. There's nothin' you can do 'cept make a nuisance of yourself, maybe. The boys took a wagon out this mornin', so they'll be gone a day or so. An' stay away from that window,' she added. 'Around here, the hills have eyes.'

Jubal took a long breath and stared up at the hanging cluster of candle lamps. Tomorrow he'd ride out. But he'd have to talk to Essie before he went. Then his thoughts turned to Hester, and he wondered if Bear Ogden had dragged himself out to the ranch. Yeah, tomorrow, he decided, and hoped Alice's platter of food would speed his mending.

A few hours later that afternoon, Kingsley Post and Pug Marley rode into Pitchfork. Marley wanted a new pair of boots, but they agreed to start from Post's own KP bar. But, after the first drink, Post excused himself, saying he had some business to attend to. Standing outside on the boardwalk, he felt the grim mood resettle over him.

Last night, Ike Cooper and his men had returned to the ranch empty-handed. Today, at noon, the posse had brought in Marley's horse with the news that Jubal Lorde had spent the night in a Rod 4 line shack. Grif Benton had asked if they should keep a few men watching the Box ranch, but Post had decided against it. He wanted to lull Hester into thinking her place would be a safe haven for Lorde. 'Kill him with kindness,' he'd said harshly.

As he made his way to the bank, a gawky young man came from the telegraph office and swung up on to a dusty mare. He neck-reined the animal and grinned at Post. 'You got me a job yet, Mr Post?' he asked, the immature grin widening.

'Not now, Lenny,' Post replied, without giving him a second glance.

Outside of the bank, the telegraph operator nodded curtly as Post brushed past him. Inside, Cosmo Horage asked Post to take a seat in his office. For a moment, they passed the time of day, before Post mentioned the loan he'd been negotiating.

The manager frowned and he rubbed his chin. 'Well, your account's pretty short at the moment, Kingsley. It's to do with the deal you made for Arnwood's place.'

'I know,' Post said impatiently. He had cash in his safe at the saloon and floats at the lumber yard and his ranch house, but they were there as working monies. 'I've got the yard an' the saloon an' the ranch. Nothin's owed, so there's a heap o' collateral. What's the problem, Cosmo?'

'Well, things ain't quite what they were. There's been some changes to—'

'Changes to what?' Post interrupted.

'Ase Linder's died. That means your land offer ain't goin' to be much more than an offer, I'm afraid.'

'How do you know he's dead?'

'I've just been told there was a telegram. It happened this mornin'. I'm sorry, Kingsley, but there's nothin' I can do.'

At the shock news, panic tore through Post. With Linder dead, his hold on Essie would be broken. He could threaten to ruin her brother's legal prospects, but it didn't have the visceral bite of what he had in mind.

'There's no reason why we can't go ahead with the loan, though,' Horage offered. 'It just means you sign one set o' papers instead o' two, if you see what I mean.'

A nervous edginess crowded in on Post. 'I'd like the cash as soon as possible,' he said, getting to his feet. 'I'll be seein' Miss Essie about Adam's Stamp. I've still got another iron in the fire.'

Post returned to the saloon to pick up Marley. He told him they had to take an important ride out of town, that he'd buy him a fine pair of stovepipe boots the next time they were there.

They rode fast, and in less than twenty minutes they saw Lenny ahead of them. He was nearing the point where the Rod 4 ranch road joined the valley road. They kicked a bit harder and were soon drawing alongside the youngster.

Lenny turned and raised his hand in greeting. 'Where you both goin'?' he asked, with the grin still in place.

'Looks like the same place as you, Lenny. We got a little business with Miss Linder.'

'I got a telegraph for her.'

Post nodded encouragingly. 'That's good, Lenny. But there's no sense in all of us takin' a ride out there,' he said. 'Why not let me deliver it?'

'Can't do that. Mr Post. It's against regulations,' Lenny said, his grin merging with a thin line of worry.

'There's no harm, Lenny, besides, no one's goin' to know. When you get back to town, go an' have a round at the KP. Say it's to go on my personal account. An' hand in your notice at the telegraph office. Startin' Monday week, there's a job at the ranch if you want it. What do you say?'

'If that's the suet, Mr Post, I'll say yes,' Lenny said, and handed over the telegram. 'Don't you go readin' it now,' he said, bringing back the grin.

Post and Marley had already turned their horses away. 'Ha, would I ever,' Post called out, waved offhandedly as they took the road to the Bar T ranch.

When they were close to the ranch buildings, but still out of sight, Post opened the telegram.

FATHER SUFFERED STROKE STOP. PASSED AWAY AT 9.15 A.M. STOP. WROTE IRIS STOP. WILL LOOK FOR YOU TO ARRIVE FIRST POSSIBLE NILLINGS CONNECTION STOP.

Slowly, Post folded the sheet of paper. Ase Linder's death meant that Essie would undoubtedly inherit the Rod 4. Iris was too young and Rex Linder cared little for the cattle business. From this day forward, there wouldn't be any more power of attorney. Essie would be running the ranch in her own right.

But nothing was lost yet. If he played his cards right, he needn't fold on his long game. He'd taken an extra chance, Now he had to move on it.

'Find somewhere to ease up them toes o' yours, Marley. Just stay out o' sight until I get back,' he said, and set off towards the Linder ranch house.

18

Leaning against the veranda handrail, Essie Linder wished that time could reverse itself. She didn't want to face Jubal, and had stayed away from the ranch on purpose. For a few miles, she'd ridden along the west bank of the creek, then she'd gone to see Hester. She thought Hester had a right to know about Jubal, but had been very surprised to meet Bear Ogden there, with his message that Jubal was safe and well enough.

Not having much choice, she'd told Hester that that was right, although Jubal was now at the Rod 4. Unsurprisingly, Hester had wanted to ride back immediately with her to see him.

Now, wondering what she was going to say to him, Essie got to her feet and paced back and forth. Should she lie, or suggest that none of it was any business of his?

She was thinking that none of it would set things to rights, when she heard the whinny of an approaching horse. She looked across the yard, moments before recognizing the rider as Kingsley Post.

As he rode up, the man looked at Hester's tethered horse with watchful interest.

'Company?' he asked as he reined in.

'Hester's stopped by.'

His gaze moved over the house and across the yard. He looked at the horse again and tugged at the lobe of an ear. 'Can't see her,' he said.

'That's because she's in the house,' Essie responded stiffly.

Post swung down from the saddle and Essie pulled a grim, considerate smile as the horse snorted.

'Where have you been?' Post asked, as he stepped up on to the veranda.

'Manners were never your strong point,' she told him. 'Just remember you're on my property an' it ain't by invitation.'

When Essie said that the ranch was her property, he faltered. But he knew it wasn't, couldn't be literal. 'An' last night?' he smirked, glancing at the front door and the windows.

'I was visitin' Hester. It's what folk do. Sometimes it's reciprocal.'

'For some reason, you're lyin', Essie, but no matter. We've got unfinished business, an' I ain't about to let a small impropriety stand in the way of our future,' Post said.

'You an' me got no future,' Essie retaliated hotly. 'That's you an' your imagination.'

'Huh. You got Jubal Lorde tucked up in there?' he said, nodding at the house.

Essie was waiting for it, and she was that less surprised. 'Yeah,' she said. 'He's in my bed. Probably got Hester with him. I'd say you've been rubbin' a bit too close to your friend Snoop Kirkland.'

Post ground his teeth, shook his head slowly. 'I might just by-pass the Denver papers . . . go straight to the dime novels. Stirrin' tales o' you an' your family should sure help your brother's legal career,' he threatened, his voice hardly above a whisper. 'I'll go in an' take a look for myself. We wouldn't want them Eastern readers to think we imagined any o' this, would we?'

Post moved towards the door, but saw he was blocked by Felix Batchelor. The man stood just inside the doorway, had a single-barrelled shotgun levelled at Post's belly.

'This ol' smoke pole will just about cut you in half, Post. So get back to that mare an' ride off,' he gritted. 'People in this neck o' the woods got good reason to be 'fear'd o' you, but me an' mine ain't. Now get off this land, you son-of-a-bitch.'

No one in the last five or six years had ever talked to him like that. But he knew the ranch foreman meant what he said.

'You an' me got unfinished business, lady, whether you like it or not,' he said, turning back to Essie. 'The consequences for your ambitious, pillar o' society brother could be disastrous. Think about livin' with that.'

Post swung himself into the saddle and heeled his horse in a swerving run across the home yard. Fifteen minutes later, Marley rode from his scrub cover to meet him. He took a long look at his boss and decided not to ask about what had happened. Post was heaving breaths and sweat coated his face.

'Lorde's there,' Post said after a full minute. 'Watch the place. They'll be movin' him tonight, an' I want to know where,' he commanded. 'I'll take the boys down to Arnwood's old place. It's closer than the ranch. Meet me there, an' make sure there's no more bunglin'.'

With Batchelor standing beside her, Essie watched until

Post disappeared along the wagon road. Then she went inside and hurried up the stairs to her bedroom that was at the back of the house.

'You'll have to leave. Post knows you're here,' she said, pushing the door open.

'You mean he suspects. Anyways, it means you comin' over to my place,' Hester offered.

Jubal swung his legs from under the covers and sat on the edge of the bed. 'How do you know this?' he asked.

'He was just here. He tried to come upstairs, but ran up against Felix an' his—'

'OK,' Jubal said. 'Hester, can you go an' saddle me a horse?'

Hester nodded, looked at Essie and gave an almost imperceptible shrug.

The moment she'd gone, Jubal turned to Essie. 'All right, Essie, now you really got to start talkin',' he said brusquely.

'We found you some trousers an' a shirt,' she started.

'I didn't mean for you to discuss my wardrobe, goddamnit. Tell me what the hell's goin' on.'

'Don't you think there's a reason I ain't told you before? Don't you think I'd have told you if I could?' she asked.

'I can't think what might be that bad, Essie. But I do know Post figures in it. So why don't you start with him?'

'It's about Pa,' Essie began slowly. 'A number of years ago he took money from a stage-line office. Post found out about it.'

Jubal stared hard at Essie for a long moment while it saink in. Then he smiled. 'Are you tellin' me your pa's an old holdup man?'

'No. He took money from the office of the stage line.

He worked there as a driver.'

Jubal continued with the smile. 'Oh, sorry, there's a difference,' he said. 'But how does that figure in what's goin' on here?'

'Post was in Denver an' got to hear about it.'

'How do you mean?'

'By chance he met Rex. It was him who sort of owned up. It was a problem he needed to get off his chest, or somethin' like that, I guess.'

Jubal shook his head nonplussed. 'An' Post came back to Pitchfork an' started to blackmail you? Is that what you're sayin'?'

'Yes. He had it worked out. He waited until Pa wasn't here, then he rode out to see me. He knew what to do with that knowledge. But Pa paid the money back, an' he knew it.'

'You never told your pa about it?' Jubal asked.

'No, it would have killed him. Rex would have been disgraced. And can you imagine what it would have been like for Iris? Schools aren't the most forgivin' of places. I gave him money to keep quiet. The price for not, was just too much. Do you understand?'

'Yeah, I understand. But there's a whole lot more than that, Essie. Seems to me it would've served your brother right for blabbin' off. An' how do you explain the death o' Billy and young Ferdie Chase?'

Essie shook her head. 'I didn't know about that, Jubal,' she claimed fiercely. 'That's why I spoke to you at the hotel. I wanted you to stay because I couldn't prove anythin'. I only suspected.'

'Well, lookin' back, those suspicions might have given me a reason to stay.'

'I'm old enough to know better than to share doubts

an' fears in a town this size,' Essie said.

'Yeah, well, here's somethin' for you, Essie,' Jubal proposed. 'If you *could* prove a case against him, would you? How many more people are goin' to suffer because o' the reputation o' you an' your family? If they come lookin for me, some are goin' to die.'

Essie gave Jubal a short, challenging look, nodded once. 'So leave, why don't you? Pack your traps an' ride away.'

Bear Ogden met Jubal and Hester as they emerged from the darkness into the yard of the Box ranch. They learned that Frank Pinner had gone to Rockford in the company of J.J. Patch, to protest the unlawful arrest of Bull McRae and the others.

Jubal swung painfully from the saddle and followed Hester into the gloom of the house. She quickly pulled the shades and lit a table lamp. Jubal looked around, saw the room was plainly furnished and very orderly, looked very clean.

Hester looked at him, asked if his leg was bleeding again.

'No, I don't think so. Brain might be though,' he tried with a weak smile.

They both felt self-conscious, as if something was about to happen, not being certain what it might be. Jubal felt the clamminess of his skin and shivered. He cursed with frustration, sat himself in a comfortable-looking, upholstered chair.

He'd only been dozing a few minutes when he woke to see Hester opening the door to an urgent knock. Toby Messenger stepped into the room, his open, freckled face sullen and angry.

'You best look for some other place to hole up,' he told Jubal. 'Post had a man watchin' Linder's place. He followed you here, an' right now he's ridin' hell bent to tell someone about it.'

'How do you know that, Toby?' Hester asked him, before Jubal had a chance.

'Because this afternoon I followed you an' Essie May to the Rod 4. I thought you were just visitin' an' I waited to ride back with you. I came to warn you, that's all.'

Jubal stretched his leg, winced at the sharp pain. 'About who?' he rasped with quiet sarcasm.

'You can stay at my place. They won't look there,' Messenger said, looking him over. 'Can you ride?'

'Unless your concern stretches to carryin' me,' Jubal said. He watched as Toby looked at Hester, grinned knowingly when she smiled back at him warmly.

'So, let's help this feller back on to his horse while we can,' Hester said. 'None of us wants to be here when the hell of Kingsley Post descends.'

'I'd say none of us wants to be anywhere when that happens,' Jubal suggested. The thought of moving again annoyed and troubled him, but he knew he couldn't stay. A gun fight would endanger more lives, and killing Post wouldn't amount to a hill of beans if he didn't confess before he died. 'But we're sure goin' to be *somewhere*,' he added dourly.

19

'A few o' you get around back,' Kingsley Post shouted, as the posse swept across the yard. Immediately, three or four of the riders circled the ranch buildings while others swung from their saddles and ran through the darkness toward the house.

'There ain't nobody here.' Grif Benton was sitting his saddle beside Post.

Post grunted, called for Pug Marley who came from the house. 'You sure this is where they came?' he demanded.

'Yeah, I'm sure,' Marley replied huffily. 'Him an' the Box girl. I told you there was someone here waitin'. I couldn't make 'em out, an' when they started for the house, I beat it.'

'Maybe they spooked an' went back to Linder's place,' Benton suggested.

'An' maybe they went to the Chase ranch, or to town,' Post added angrily.

Benton edged his horse close alongside Post. 'I guess you never saw fit to tell me what's really goin' on here,' he said quietly. 'But I'm beginnin' to think this Lorde feller has got you by the pecker.'

Post didn't answer. He wasn't yet prepared to reveal his scheme, or admit to his foreman-come-hired gun that he was a blackmailer with something on Essie Linder.

'You're right, the place is deserted,' he said a few moments later. 'Take the boys to Arnwood's place. I'm goin' on to town, an' I'll see you later.'

Solitary and thoughtful, Post cantered across the open range and picked up the valley road. He was in a spot. There were too many loose ends. If the news of Ase Linder's death reached Essie, there would be hell to pay. Either Essie, or someone close to her, was helping Lorde, but there was little doubt she'd given the man refuge at her ranch.

Post ground his teeth until his jaw ached. Tomorrow he would make her a proposition, and this time it would be final; no more belligerence at every turn.

He was still in a dark mood when he rode into town. As he walked his horse across the entrance to piss alley and the honky-tonks, a voice hailed him. It spooked him and he cursed his unease.

'You give Miss Essie that telegram?' the telegraph operator called out.

'Yeah, of course I gave it to her.' Post's response conveyed the anger and unease he felt at the thought of young Lenny, talking.

'I was only askin' . . . meant no harm,' the man said. 'You got to be careful about spreadin' news if it ain't from the recipient. I guess she told you what it said?'

'Yeah, she did. It's a shame. A real shame,' Post replied with little obvious feeling.

The man nodded. 'I been down to the depot. Figured she'd be catchin' the late stage up to Lovell Station, only she never showed.'

Post gripped the saddle horn with irritation and cursed under his breath. 'That's because I offered to drive her some o' the way, early tomorrow,' he said, trying not to show he'd been caught off guard.

'Ah, that'll be all right then,' the telegraph operator said. 'Otherwise that durned kid could've been in real trouble.' He bade Post good day, and moved on up the street,

Post took a deep breath, forced himself to stay calm, hold his nerve. It was nothing more than a close shave, but the hole was getting deeper. He swore again. Lies layering lies was getting to be an onerous burden.

He swung down in front of his saloon and hitched his horse. As usual he stopped just inside the doors for a moment to gaze around the room, weigh up the few customers. He nodded at one of the saloon girls, but she turned away moodily. When he caught the eye of Hirkam Jeffs, he got the impression the marshal had been waiting for him. He went over to the table, pulled back a chair and Jeffs nodded.

'We just missed him,' Post said. 'He was holed up at the Box place, but skipped out ahead of us.'

Jeffs made a gruff, lack of concern sound. 'Bull McRae an' his crew have been turned out,' he said.

'Turned out? You mean freed? Why?' Post asked, clearly taken aback.

'Because Frank Pinner came in this mornin' with J.J. Patch. But no one needed an attorney to establish them boys were at the Hump Rib the night o' the raid. We *all* knew, goddamn it.'

'So what happened?'

'They rode to Rockford an' got a release writ. McRae an' the Cranes have been free men for a good hour now,' Jeffs explained. 'Furthermore, in a day or two, we're gettin' a full-time deputy sheriff. As far as I'm concerned, that won't be a day too soon.'

Post shrugged. 'Well, we're both pushin' at the same door, Hirk. But the way things were, we had to do somethin', wouldn't you say?'

'Maybe. But you better get your crew back to 'punchin' cattle. An' break up that posse. Some say it looks more like a goddamn lynch party.' With that, the marshal drained his glass and took his leave. The worry returned to grip Post's stomach. He knew that if they got hold of Lorde tomorrow, he wouldn't live to see the next sunset. And what if Essie told Lorde the truth?

He went to his office and poured a stiff drink. But instead of taking a pull, he put the glass down and opened the safe. He took out and unlocked a metal box, bit his lip at the sight of the tightly packed wad of bills.

There was a knock at the door and he put the box back in the safe and pushed the door to. He sat at his desk, picked up his glass and said for whoever it was to come in. Then he cursed to himself and made an involuntary movement for his Colt when he saw the man standing before him.

'Well, Owen Chase as I live an' breathe,' he said affably. 'What are you doin' here? I thought you were snugged away in your sick bed.'

Chase's black frock coat was open enough for Post the see the handle of the Colt above the man's belt. He looked at Post with eyes that held little warmth or friendship.

'I come to see if you had any news on Jubal Lorde,' he said.

'We almost had him,' Post answered with a tremor of uncertainty. 'I'm certain the boys will bring him in tomorrow.'

'Make sure he's brought in alive.' Chase pulled the front of his coat closed, turned and went out.

Post sank down in the chair, grabbed his whiskey and downed it too quick. 'Well done, Benton,' he choked out. 'You created us another problem.'

After leaving his office, he maintained his routine of checking the cash behind the bar, and within minutes was spurring his horse from the end of town. He took the wagon road, raced to his ranch as if he were being chased by the hounds of hell.

20

Bear Ogden whistled, then called out not to shoot as he rode across Toby Messenger's yard.

'They came an' went,' he said. 'They're stayin' the night at Arnwood's old place. In the mornin' they're goin' to search the valley.'

'How the hell do you know all that, Bear?' Toby asked, as he beckoned the huge mountain man into his house.

'By gettin' real close,' Ogden replied with a sly grin. 'Post went to town, but he's due back.'

'This'll be one o' the first places they hit,' Jubal said grimly. 'An' we'll be here waitin' for 'em.' He turned to Hester and Toby. 'But you two had better get to where it's safe. So far you ain't part o' the fight.'

Toby shook his head. 'Sorry Jubal, but this is my home. An' if that ain't safe enough, where is?'

'An' are you forgettin' Billy?' Hester added. 'But I am worried about Essie. Maybe I'll ride over an' see her. They won't be watchin' her place now.'

'Perhaps they'll get tired o' trailin' me an' go home,' Jubal suggested drily. 'An' perhaps tomorrow won't be another day,' he quietly tagged on the end. He understood the concern about Essie. But he hadn't mentioned what Alice Batchelor had told him – that Post was considering marriage with Essie. That was too close to personal and private business.

'Did you an' Essie have words?' Hester asked, as if the thought just struck her.

Jubal was about to ask her what she meant, when they heard the dull thud of hoofs across the yard. Jubal blew out the lamp and drew his Colt, stood alongside the window.

Peering through the darkness for a few moments he saw and recognized four riders. 'Unprime your pieces, it's Frank Pinner,' he said with quiet relief. 'He's brought Bull an' the others.' He quickly relit the lamp, and Ogden and Toby went out to welcome the reinforcements.

Pinner and the others came inside, their features severe and drawn with tiredness.

'We've rode most o' Wyomin' before comin' here,' he said. 'What the blue blazes is goin' on?'

For a couple of minutes, Jubal explained most of what had happened. 'So from what Bear found out, they'll likely be here by mornin',' he concluded.

'Well don't go countin' on it,' Pinner advised. 'You'll more'n likely get your fight, Jubal. We all will, but it ain't likely to be here.'

'Why not?'

'Stands to reason,' Pinner replied. 'If Post went to town, like Bear said, Jeffs will see him there, an' tell him that his rag-bag of a posse ain't legal. The man's in too deep to go makin' a clear enemy o' the law, specially with a deputy on the way.'

'He'll have one last go at nailin' me,' Jubal predicted. 'You can bet your jingle bobs on that. An' I'm in no mood to frustrate his efforts.'

'That goes for all of us, Jube,' Bull McRae said. 'We got ourselves a little account to settle with some of his boys, They roughed us up before they got us to jail.'

'All of us are thinkin' o' Billy an' the Chase boy,' Pinner muttered. 'But Post's got to make the first move. If he doesn't, we wait for the deputy. What do you say?'

'It suits me, 'cause Kingsley Post ain't goin' to wait for anythin',' Jubal said. 'Now let's look to our guns.'

At dawn, a rooster crowed, and the rising sun lifted above the Wind River Mountains, threw long fingers of early light across the valley.

A rider came pounding down the slope of the basin and, from the house, the doughty defenders saw it was Bear Ogden returning.

'They're headed this way,' he said with unrestrained excitement, as he slid from the saddle of his lathered horse.

The men sniffed and coughed, as they levered shells into the chambers of their rifles, grunted with anticipation, as they looked out to where the approaching horsemen would show against the sky.

'We all know what to expect, so let's spread,' Jubal said. 'Bull, you Dan an' Frank hold the house. The rest of us will dig in around here.'

They had packed the horses into the open-sided shed between the house and the corral. There was another outhouse close by, but none of the buildings obscured the view of the slope.

'We'll do as Frank says,' Jubal said. 'No shootin' until they fire first. Maybe they'll want to talk.'

'Yeah, an' maybe they want to thumb noses, an' throw stones at my windows,' Toby retorted.

Jubal watched the crest of the slope, thankful that Hester was out of it. Toby had ridden with her to the Linder place, and had returned shortly after Bear Ogden. Jubal imagined he must have had himself a hard time making up his mind about helping him – presuming too much about his relationship with Hester.

In the middle of his musings about what was real and what wasn't, a rider appeared on the crest of the long slope. Two more joined the first, then more until he counted fourteen riders in all.

'How many do you make it?' he called out.

'Fourteen. Just about two to one,' Toby called back. 'Let's hope they ain't got a reserve company the other side of the crest.'

'Here they come,' Frank Pinner shouted from the house.

The horsemen formed a line, came down the slope at a resolute trot. When they reached a near to halfway point, the riders drew rein, and Jubal recognized Post on his big grey.

'They're thinkin' it out,' Ogden muttered. 'I reckon they know we're down here.'

Jubal had a look around him. Toby was at the end of the corral, Erskine Crane near the shed, both with levelled rifles. Ogden stood near Jubal, his head forward, eyes squinting into the sunlight.

'Remember, no shootin' until they do,' Jubal called out. 'It'll count for us if this get-together ever reaches court.'

'I reckon this is our court, Jubal,' Toby shouted back. 'Looks like they do mean to talk,' he added, as Post and the others continued down the slope at a measured walk.

'We can do that,' Jubal said thoughtfully, and more to himself.

Toby swore as the riders trampled across a corner of his bean patch. 'If they ain't makin' a charge, you'd think they'd ride around,' he said angrily.

With a rifle across the pommel of his saddle, Post rode ahead. Grif Benton kept pace on his left and John Tolliver was to his right.

'Keep an eye on Benton,' Jubal said. 'He's Post's gun hand, an' gettin' paid for it. That an' other things.'

'Step forward, Lorde,' Tolliver called out. 'You're the one we came for.'

'You here to arrest me?' Jubal shouted back.

'You ain't got no jurisdiction outside o' the town limits, Tolliver,' Toby shouted from the house. 'An' in case Post didn't tell you, Bull McRae an' the boys are out o' jail. Lawyer Patch got a release order, an' right now they've all got rifles trained on your gut.'

Tolliver immediately turned to Post. 'You didn't tell me about no court order,' he challenged furiously.

'Just get Lorde out here,' Post snapped.

'Post pay you some graft too, did he, Deputy?' Ogden then jeered. 'Best watch out though. Let him down, an' you could be forkin' clouds with Kirkland an' Sand.'

Post hadn't seen Bear Ogden. Now he stared as the big man edged a step sideways into the open. 'I thought you'd run to the hills after that beatin' Lorde gave you,' he said, taken aback.

'You thought wrong,' Ogden growled and spat.

Post spoke to Tolliver quietly and the man nodded, and faced the yard,

'We're after Lorde, an' we want no trouble from the rest o' you,' the deputy town marshal said. 'Either you step forward or we come an' get you.'

'Think about that, Tolliver,' Jubal warned. 'In a couple

o' days, when the deputy sheriff gets here, I'll still be alive, but you'll be dead. Unlike you an' yours, these fellers are loyal to a fault.'

Tolliver turned to Post a second time. 'For Chris'sakes, you never told me there was a county sheriff comin' here,' he seethed. 'What the hell else ain't you mentioned?'

Post said something and Tolliver shook his head, reluctantly.

'We'll see him safe in jail. He can await trial,' he called out, his hopes of a capture fading.

'Hah, who are you tryin' to fool?' Toby shouted back. 'He'd never see the inside of any jail, an' you know it.'

'Nobody asked you, dirt grubber,' Post retorted. He started to swing up his rifle but he lowered it slowly as he caught sight of Jubal.

'Hey, Post. You can't pay us all off, the way you did me with a bottle o' rotgut whiskey. Or the way you paid Sand an' Kirkland an' me to rustle your cattle,' Ogden contributed to the battle of words. 'That's right, now all of us know the truth o' your business.'

This time, Post did use his rifle. He took a snap shot at Ogden and the bullet splintered a corral post.

But the moment Ogden spoke up, Jubal had seen it coming. 'Hold your fire, all o' you,' he shouted. 'Can't blame him, he's just a tad spiky.' When no return gunfire came from the house, he called out again. 'You've been ummin' an' aaghin' for too long, Post. Now state your case or call off the show. Make up your mind.'

Post swore and wheeled his horse. Tolliver hesitated, then he and Benton followed back up the slope.

When they reached the spot where they'd halted first time round, all the men dismounted and gathered around Post. After a short parley, they started back for Messenger's yard on foot, half of them circled wide to come in behind the ranch buildings. One man kneeled and fired and Jubal heard the overhead whine of the bullet. Another put a bullet through a window. Jubal took careful aim on a running man, lined him up and squeezed off his shot. The man stumbled, ran on a bit, then sprawled forward and lay still.

'Thirteen,' Jubal called out.

'Yeah, an unlucky number,' Toby responded, and issued a grim, grating chuckle. 'We're gettin' our fight, that's for sure.'

'Yeah,' Jubal agreed as he got down flat to the ground. 'An' they started it.'

21

Jubal gritted his teeth at the pain in his legs as he squinted along the barrel of his rifle. Sweat ran down his forehead, into his eyes as he fired. He heard the howl from the man who ran for the shelter of the outhouse.

There were two dead men in the yard. After the initial exchange of gunfire, when they'd tried to rush the corral, one of Post's men lay sprawled on his back, another lay face down, clawing the hard-packed dirt. The man Jubal had shot on the slope had crawled out of sight.

Nobody in the house had been hit, and of those around the corral, Erskine Crane had suffered an arm wound, but he was still able to hold a gun.

Post's crew had fared the worst. They'd had very little cover, and most of them were now heads down in the irrigation ditch that ran from the creek to the edge of the yard.

Eventually, Jubal spotted Post. He was riding his grey up the slope towards his crew's horses. This was the first time Jubal had seen the man since the shooting started, and he wondered what he was up to. He decided that Post must be thinking that sooner or later, someone would be riding out to see what was happening. The news would race back to Pitchfork, and that was something that Post could ill afford.

Someone fired a single shot, but Jubal didn't know who was involved until he heard the shout from Toby Messenger.

'I think I winged me a goddamn deputy marshal,' he called out.

Jubal continued to ponder on Post's dilemma, tried to put himself in the man's shoes. The so-called businessman was in a tight spot. Seeing Bear Ogden had shaken him, provoked him into firing the first shot. Then it was too late, and pride had likely goaded him to try and finish what he'd started.

'Twixt the hammer an' the anvil, Mr Post,' Jubal said aloud. He gave a twisted grin at the thought of how much worse Post would feel if he knew that Essie had talked, and that it was she who'd fired at him from the ridge above his house. But Jubal was aware that there was still no compelling proof against Post. Bear Ogden's testimony about the rustling wouldn't carry much weight with both Sand and Kirkwood being dead. Still, it was hurtful stuff, and Post had made a mistake in not getting rid of Ogden as he had the other two.

Jubal scanned the yard. There was nothing to shoot at or get shot by, and five more uneventful minutes went by until Bear Ogden yelled that there was a rider approaching. He raised himself painfully, then moved forward at a limping crouch across the corral. He looked out towards the cedar stand, saw the rider coming from the direction of the creek. He wiped the sweat from his eyes, then standing, he shouted back.

'Don't fire. It's Essie Linder.'

As if to avoid an interception, Essie was swerving her

horse in wide arcs. Jubal put his rifle across the top rail, centred it on Kingsley Post as the man spurred his horse from cover of the timber.

Essie entered the yard at a full gallop. She drew rein in a cloud of dust, turned to look back at Post, who was trailing her at a watchful canter.

'Come an' join the party,' she called out. 'Everyone's got to hear this.'

Post's men raised themselves from their cover, but they didn't come forward. Bull McRae, Frank Pinner and Daniel Crane walked from the house, and Benton and Tolliver eased in from the same direction. Jubal saw that Tolliver had his left arm inside his shirt, that was stained dark with blood.

'What the hell are you doin' here?' Post's voice was harsh and threatening.

Pinner came forward and looked up at Essie's determined face. 'You got somethin' to say, miss, just say it. You sure got a captive audience,' he encouraged.

Essie's jaw worked a bit before she spoke. 'Post's been blackmailin' me,' she said.

'Goddamnit, Essie May, you best be sure o' what you're sayin',' Post hissed out dangerously.

'I'm makin' sure of a lot o' things,' Essie ripped back. 'It was *you* who had Billy Box killed. An' you who planned an' carried out the raid.'

Eager to witness a new drama, the men on both sides were pressing closer across the yard.

'That'll be enough from you, lady,' Benton gruffed. But then he turned towards Post. 'Looks like you been called, boss. What happens now?'

Post's face was a mask of fury. 'She's lyin' . . . can't prove a goddamn thing.'

Benton looked puzzled. 'That ain't my problem, boss,' he said. 'I want to know what we're to do now.'

'If I was you, I'd ride away,' Jubal, joined in. 'Post can hang himself when we get him to court.'

Post sat motionless on his big grey horse, wrath and doubt taking turns to disfigure his face.

'You just stay put, cowboy,' Benton told Jubal, then he looked back at Post. 'I reckon some of us might have to make tracks,' he said, as though he'd been reading Jubal's thoughts.

Post still didn't respond. He hunched his shoulders, as though figuring out where he stood and what he could do about it. He switched his attention between Essie and Jubal.

'You sure you don't want to think this out?' he asked of Essie. 'You know what it'll mean.'

'I already have, an' it means you won't be hurtin' me any more,' she said steadily.

Benton shook his head. 'Whatever you came here to start, I reckon it's just ended,' he directed at Post.

During the next heavy silence, Jubal saw that John Tolliver was edging his way up the slope, back towards the horses. A second man started after him, and the rest were stirring impatiently. To Jubal it looked as though whatever force had kept them there was loosening its grip.

'The hell with this,' Pug Marley said, breaking the silence. He turned his back on the corral and ranch house and started walking up the slope. Ike Cooper hesitated, then shrugged and followed.

Post looked around at the rest of his men, gave no sign that the others had gone. 'Their horses are in that shed,' he said. 'Turn 'em loose . . . send em out on a run.'

Ogden shifted beside Jubal. He muttered angrily and

took a step forward.

'Stay where you are, Bear. An' that goes for the rest of you. Just let 'em go,' Jubal snapped. He still had Post cold, but Benton had Essie, and wasn't too far off shooting her at a word from Post.

The sun crept higher into the sky and Essie's horse jerked its head up, snorted and pawed restlessly at the ground.

'Climb down, lady,' Benton commanded.

'Better do as he tells you, Essie,' Jubal said when Essie hesitated. 'For a man who's taken on Peepin' Toms an' town drunks, defenceless girls are well within his capability.'

Benton snorted. 'I won't mess her up too much,' he retorted with a mean grin. 'But a man like me always needs insurance.'

The rest of Post's men began to move away up the slope. Those who'd gone ahead, had already reached their horses and were making tracks in the direction of the KP ranch.

Benton pushed Essie's horse to one side before mounting it. 'Start walkin',' he said, indicating the slope with the barrel of his rifle.

Post still hadn't moved. 'I'll be seein' you later,' he said, as Benton rode past him.

'An' I know where,' Benton replied.

'The same goes for you, Lorde,' Post continued. 'Give you somethin' to look forward to.' Then he broke off, as though a sudden thought had struck him 'Hold up, Benton,' he said.

'Yeah?' Benton asked. He kept his rifle pointed at Essie who'd stopped a few paces ahead of him.

'Just remembered I've got somethin' here for Essie,'

Post said, lifting his hand slowly from his coat pocket.

Jubal's finger tightened on the trigger, and his heart hammered against his ribs. He wondered what Benton would do if he shot Post. But he knew he couldn't take the chance.

Post was held out a square of paper, then he skimmed it towards Essie. 'Someone should've delivered this a lot earlier,' he said maliciously.

Jubal watched as Essie walked back and picked up the telegram. She read it, and he saw her choke on a cry of terrible grief. Her legs buckled as she stumbled away, and he drew back the hammer of his rifle and turned on Post.

Post threw up a restraining hand. 'You pull that trigger, an' Benton will put a bullet in her before you get one in me,' he said. 'An' now I'm ridin' out o' here.'

'Either one o' you lays a hand on her, I'll hunt you down,' Jubal pledged gravely.

Post spurred his horse out of the yard, towards the valley's wagon road. Benton and Essie were moving across the slope where a rider with a spare horse was coming to meet them. Essie mounted up, and the three riders single-footed up to the rim of the basin.

Jubal lowered his rifle and crossed the yard. There wasn't a horse left on the ranch, and he was in no condition to walk further than the home pasture.

He walked stiffly over to Bull McRae and the others. As he reached them he stopped and turned to where they were pointing. Toby Messenger issued a cry of greeting and ran forward. McRae looked to Jubal and shrugged bemusedly because they'd seen Hester Box riding up from the creek.

22

Kingsley Post spurred his big grey along the valley road. Confused, nervous thoughts were flashing through his mind when he saw the rider waiting ahead of him. As he reined in, John Tolliver levelled his Colt.

'Don't try anythin' slick,' he said.

'Tolliver? What the hell are you doin' here?' Post questioned.

'Thinkin' to my future.'

Though Tolliver's left arm had been hit, he gripped the reins with that hand, and Post guessed it wasn't much of a wound.

'What's wrong with you?' he demanded. 'Put that gun away, goddamnit.'

'Not yet. I don't think you're a man to be totally trusted,' Tolliver responded. 'So I'm forkin' out o' here, an' before that deputy sheriff arrives. I ain't in no mood for any fancy exchange with a jury.'

Post gave a short, barking laugh. 'You already said you know nothin',' he reminded the deputy marshal. 'Besides, nobody's got anythin' on you *or* me.'

'Hah, the hell they haven't,' Tolliver answered back. 'I know you planned the raid, an' now I'm thinkin' it was *you* who had Sand an' Kirkland killed.'

Post studied Tolliver a moment, trying to assess the man's intention.

'I've always done your biddin', Mr Post, but I ain't done that well by it,' Tolliver continued. 'So, if any lawman does get to me, I might be bringin' him right to your front door.'

Post saw that Tolliver was gripping his Colt purposefully, knew it was too late to push for any sort of deal. 'What is it you want?' he asked.

Tolliver nodded, gestured with the gun. 'That's more like it. I'll gamble you're packin' enough to keep me happy. Let's take a look.'

Post's nerves twitched as he took out his wallet and fingered the bills. 'There's more'n three hundred dollars, here,' he said. 'Where's that goin' to take you?'

Tolliver reached for the bulky wallet and quickly stuffed it in his shirt pocket. 'Somewhere I can expect to live a little longer than if I stay here.' Then he indicated that Post ride on. 'An' stay away from that sheriff,' he warned sarcastically.

Tolliver sat his horse thoughtfully, waited awhile before he took out Post's wallet. He counted a little over $200, shook his head and made a sound of disgust. No wonder I never made full marshal, he thought. Then he touched his horse with a spur and followed Post towards town.

Jubal Lorde had urged Hester Box's flagging horse up the long slope. The moment he crossed the rim he saw the three riders ahead of him. They rode non-stop past the Box ranch buildings, then swung right to pick up the valley road.

Jubal figured they would cross the road and make a

beeline for Post's ranch. Cleaving the range, a long jagged spike of rock rose dark against the landscape, and with luck, he could reach it ahead of them.

After riding hard for another twenty minutes, he managed to circle the unsuspecting riders. He dismounted and stood with his back against an angle of the rocky outcrop. His breathing was heavy and his thigh was throbbing with a fearsome hurt. He was sweating profusely and the light in front of his eyes danced with sparkling, white spots.

Five minutes later, the sound of muffled hoofbeats reached him. He wiped the sweat from his eyes and levered a shell into the chamber of his rifle. Lowering his head he took a cautious look at the approaching riders. He cursed, blinked hard to clear his vision, cursed again at the sight of Essie riding between Grif Benton and Ike Cooper.

Jubal watched them ride up the slope, wiped his sleeve across his face as they got closer. He leaned into the rock face and felt its heat against his chest, thought it might be the run of his fever. He looked again and raised his rifle, He wasn't going to fool around with the likes of Benton, but then again, he wasn't going to shoot the man without a warning.

'Not like they did against young Billy,' he muttered, as he raised the rifle barrel and cradled the stock against his shoulder.

'That's far enough. Rein in,' he challenged, when they were nearly upon him. 'Essie, you ride clear,' he added quickly.

Benton had moved the moment Jubal called out. He pulled his gun and spurred his horse into a tight, swerving turn. His gun blasted, but the bullet struck rock and whined off into space. Calmly, Jubal tracked him, held his breath before squeezing the trigger. He hit Benton in the side. The man shuddered, then started to fall, then pulled himself up again.

'Didn't think you'd go easy,' Jubal said, and fired again. This time, Benton rolled forward, collapsed to the ground and lay still.

Crouched low in the saddle, Cooper was racing back down the slope. Jubal sighted carefully and fired. He heard the thump of the bullet, saw the horse stumble and go down. Cooper tumbled clear then scrambled to his feet. He was dragging at his holstered Colt, looked towards Jubal, as he ran for the rocks at his right.

'There ain't much safety *there*,' Jubal said and pulled the trigger once again.

Cooper took the bullet high in the side of his chest, was dead before he hit the ground.

Jubal was already moving, pushing himself from cover of the rocks. 'I need your horse, Essie,' he called. 'I'm meetin' someone in Pitchfork.'

Essie dismounted, looked around as if she was expecting more men to emerge from the very ground.

'It's all right. You've rode in an' out of all the trouble there's goin' to be,' Jubal consoled her. 'There won't be any more.'

'Are you goin' to leave me here alone?' she asked with plain fear.

'No. I'm not leavin' you anywhere. The horse I was ridin's tied into the rocks just below here. It's just about all in, but it'll get you to Hester's place. I'll be along later, don't worry.'

Essie gazed at him. 'Did you have to kill them?' she asked, apparently still shocked.

Jubal cursed under his breath. 'Can you think of anythin' better?' he retorted. 'It's what they would've done to me . . . us.'

Grinding his teeth against the pain, Jubal mounted again. He made a wide circle, looked down at Benton.

Kingsley Post's dying gunman blinked his eyes against the sun. 'Wouldn't be so bad if I knew you were goin' to smoke the boss,' he said.

'You got my solemn word on that,' Jubal pledged. 'But don't quit on me just yet, I got somethin' to ask you,' he said. 'Was it Sand who shot my friend, Billy Box?'

'Yeah, an' I gutted *him*. Guess I done you a favour,' Benton rasped as a final thought.

'Thanks. Life's about give an' take,' Jubal replied pitilessly. Then he punched the horse's neck, told it to hammer for town.

23

Kingsley Post eased up as he entered town, slowed his lathered horse to a walk. Once he glanced back and saw John Tolliver about a quarter of a mile behind him. When he looked again, the man was turning from the main street to the Hump Rib Hotel.

A man called out to Post from the boardwalk, and an unusual sense of relief rushed through him. It was obvious that some of the townsfolk hadn't heard what had happened out at Toby Messenger's ranch. But it got him to thinking about how much time he had left. Would they be after him right away, or would they leave him until the deputy sheriff arrived from Rockford?

He continued on towards the bank, gave a short, nervous laugh as he rode past his KP saloon.

'You're a little early,' Cosmo Horage, said. 'We're just workin' up the papers. Be another half-hour or so before there's anythin' to sign.'

'So, I'll be back,' Post responded curtly as he strode from the manager's office. He stood outside on the boardwalk, for a moment. A half-hour wait for $10,000? Yeah, just about worth the gamble, he grinned deviously. He rode to the lumber yard for what money there was in the cash box, then to the livery stable where he had his buggy harnessed. By the time they started looking for him, he'd be well on the way to making a connection with the Yellowstone Flyer.

He had connections in Miles City and, once there, he'd have little to fear. He'd keep his head down for a while, take the opportunity to ponder on whether treading water with a money bag was better than sinking with a safe.

He drove the buggy to the yard out back of his saloon. He entered the building through a side door, and went straight to the till behind the bar counter. Out of habit he checked the register, then took all the bills and most of the gold coin.

His bartender told him that Hirkam Jeffs was looking for him.

'Did he say what he wanted?' Post asked, pushing home the till drawer.

'No. He said he was lookin' for Tolliver as well. What's goin' on?'

Nothin' for you to worry about,' Post replied. 'Where did he go?'

The bartender shrugged. 'Somewhere. His horse was just outside.'

Post went to his office. It looked like maybe Jeffs was getting suspicious of his deputy. But it only mattered if Jeffs ran into Tolliver before the man left town, and Tolliver decided for one reason or another to come out with the truth. He hurriedly unlocked the safe and filled a leather satchel with the money. Then he looked around the room, felt a rising bitterness at the fact that he was running out.

As he turned the buggy from the yard, he glanced back, swallowed his thoughtful curses. His moody saloon girl was watching him from a rear upper window, and for a moment their eyes locked, perceptively. Post snapped the lines and rode away, but he knew the girl had him down in her brand book.

24

Riding into town on Essie's horse, Jubal noticed the buggy parked out front of the bank, but he didn't know it belonged to Post. He rode straight to the marshal's office, but found it empty. When he called out, the aged cleaner stepped blearily from the bunk room.

'Marshal ain't here. He's out looking for his deputy,' she said.

Jubal nodded. 'Yeah, well, I'm lookin' for Kingsley Post,' he muttered to himself. 'He'd better start doin' the same.'

Jubal wasn't about to take the law into his own hands, but unless he could find Post and hold him in custody, he had little choice. As he rode back along the street, passing riders nodded uneasily in his direction, and folk along the boardwalks dealt him questioning stares.

At the corner of piss alley, he dismounted unhurriedly in front of Post's saloon. He stood for a little while, waiting for the pain to ebb. He was weary and his mind was more on Essie Linder, than Kingsley Post. He took a few rapid, short breaths, forced her from his thoughts and entered the saloon.

The bartender was drumming his fingers on the bar, frowning at the cash register. He looked up as Jubal limped across the room and he mumbled something under his breath.

'You look like the feller who lost a quarter, an' found a' dime,' he suggested in a friendly enough manner.

'Yeah, somethin' like that,' the bartender said, and gave Jubal an old-fashioned look.

'Is Post around?' Jubal asked.

'No.'

'I'll bet you've been trained to say that,' Jubal retorted. 'But it don't matter.' He held up his hand in a manner that suggested it would be unwise for the bartender to follow, and went to the office. He drew his Colt and flung open the door.

'It's true,' he muttered, as he looked indifferently around Post's empty office.

'He left about ten minutes ago,' the dark-haired saloon girl said, when he turned around.

'Shut it,' the bartender warned. 'If you want to keep your job, get back to work.'

'Hah, there won't be a job for much longer. Not for me or anyone who works in this cess pit,' the girl said resentfully. 'I saw him leave, an' he weren't carryin' no overnight bag. It was a plump purse an' he was drivin' his rig.'

Jubal nodded his thanks, gave a stiff but genuine smile along with it.

'Good riddance, I say,' the girl said, as Jubal pushed his way out through the front doors. He looked along the street, and outside of the bank stood the matched bays of Post's rig.

Jubal patted the rump of his horse, then crossed over towards the bank where sunlight glittered on one of the town's dust free windows. He shaded his eyes and peered inside, saw a clerk and three or four customers. There was no sign of Kingsley Post.

He entered the bank, checked out the door at one end of the room. The clerk looked up from behind the dark, polished counter and Jubal indicated the door with a jerk of his head.

'Is Post in there?' he asked.

'With Mr Horage,' the clerk said with a quick nod. 'If you take a seat . . . or would you rather stand,' he said, noticing Jubal's bloodstained trousers.

'Thanks, but standin's best for what I got to do,' he said. Then he drew his Colt and made straight for the manager's door. He steadied himself for a moment, then in one movement opened the door and stepped across the threshold into the office.

Behind the desk, Cosmo Horage stared up at him pleadingly, because Post had him covered from the nearside corner of the room.

'Come in an' close the door,' Post advised steadily. 'I saw you cross the street . . . didn't think you was headed for a wash an' brush up.'

'What's this all about?' Horage said in a shaky voice.

Sweat began to run down Post's taut features. 'Just do what I say, Lorde,' he rasped. 'Start by droppin' that hogleg, or I'll put a bullet into nice Mr Horage.'

Jubal knew that Post must be in a tight enough spot to carry out his threat. He could take a chance and shoot Post, but it meant making a half turn, and even Post would have adequate time to shoot Horage. He dropped his gun.

'Get over there by the window,' Post commanded. 'Now, listen to me, Cosmo,' he continued. 'I want you to get up an' walk out o' here. I want you to climb into that buggy out front, an' pick up the reins. I'll be behind you all the way, an' if I don't like what you're doin', I'll kill you.'

Horage had his hands flat on the desk, was staring at Post as though he couldn't believe the predicament he was in. Jubal was thinking that Post had got a very good chance of getting away.

'If you're figurin' on a get-together with Benton, you'll be ridin' a hell of a ways to do it,' he said with chilling deliberation. He paused to let the implication sink in. 'I know he killed Ralph Sand, an' I'm guessin' it was him who done for Kirkland. Knowin' *why*, ain't such a guess.'

Post scowled, but didn't commit himself. He stooped and picked up Jubal's Colt, pushed it inside his belt and put his own gun in his coat pocket. 'You know so much, perhaps you can tell me why I didn't get him to kill you while he was at it,' he said.

'Because with your background you know the odds,' Jubal retaliated.

Post sneered. 'Get up, Cosmo,' he said. 'Let's go.'

The bank manager looked a badly bewildered man as he came around the desk.

'If you want this man to live, you'll stay right here until we're out o' town,' Post warned Jubal, 'Remember, do exactly like I told you,' he then said to Horage and moved the gun in his pocket.

Horage gave Jubal a frightened look and opened the door. He stepped out and Post followed, the money satchel was in his left hand, and his right held the gun in his coat pocket. The moment the door closed, Jubal moved. His helpless rage dropped away as he limped around the desk to the second door. He opened it and went down a narrow hallway that opened on to a side alley.

Almost dragging his bad leg, he went into a scuttling,

tortured run towards the main street. 'Final settlement, Billy,' he muttered, sensing the end was fast approaching. 'An' for you, Wes. An' no more goddamn blackmail, Essie,' he grated, as at last the adrenalin started to course through his veins.

He ran on and turned into the main street. He saw a group of horses at a hitch rail, grunted at the sight of a carbine stock projecting from a saddle boot.

He drew out the gun and levered a round into the chamber, made it as fast as he could to the next corner. Paying no attention to the startled looks from the townsfolk who were passing by, he got to within thirty feet of where Post's KP saloon cornered piss alley. Then he saw the rig. Horage was ham-fistedly holding the reins, and Post was sitting very close on his far side.

Jubal knew what a difficult shot it would be to make. If he missed Post, he'd probably hit some blameless citizen on the opposite boardwalk. And if he did hit the man, Post would instinctively shoot through his pocket and kill Horage.

Jubal cursed savagely for a second or two, then, it all happened for him.

25

As Jubal raised his carbine, a man shouted from the boardwalk. Horace wrenched at the reins, and the horses panicked at the sudden harsh control. They swerved violently, lunged into their traces as the nearside wheel of the rig hit a roadside trough. The vehicle collapsed, its axle on Post's side digging into the hard-packed dirt of the street. One bay stumbled to its knees. It dragged its partner to its haunches and the buggy ground to a violent, raucous stop.

Jubal watched as Horage got to his feet and scrambled up on to the boardwalk. Then he looked back at Post, and took aim.

'There's no where else to go, Post,' he shouted. 'It's all run out.'

Post twisted away from the fallen rig, and made a diagonal run for the nearest side street. Jubal groaned with frustration and set himself for an accurate sighting. He was about to squeeze the trigger when someone who was frantically scuttling for cover blundered between him and the target.

'Somebody stop him,' Horage was now yelling. 'He's got money.'

'I'm tryin', for God's sake,' Jubal rasped out. He crouched down, turned around the corner building, and saw Post at the end of the alley. He fired, but it was too agitated a shot, and he missed his target. Post flattened himself against the side of a building, and returned fire as Jubal threw himself to the ground.

Then Post was running again. Jubal cursed and got to his feet as Post slipped into the narrow street that ran to the end of piss alley. The cornered man was running towards the back entrance of his KP saloon, and Jubal plunged after him.

'I forgot. When there's nowhere else to go, try home, eh Post?' he rasped while levering up another shell. He wasn't going to catch Post now, and his leg wasn't letting him go much further. 'Make a stand, you son-of-a-bitch,' he shouted in despair.

As if he'd heard the challenge, Post stopped outside the saloon's back door, At bay, he finally turned to face his adversary.

Jubal's legs stumbled him forward another few paces. But he was off balance and lurching straight into the range of Post's gun. As he fell, he slid his right hand down the stock of the carbine. He gasped in pain as he landed hard in the dirt, sprawled forward with the carbine ahead of him. But he brought the gun up in the same motion, levelled it on the target ahead of him. It was a drill he'd learned while scouting for the cavalry, mopping up renegade Indians.

He heard the blast of Post's Colt, but he didn't see it. He supported the barrel of the carbine in the palm of his hand, and pocketed the butt in his shoulder. He steadied the blade of the front sight on Post's waistcoat and squeezed the trigger.

'Real fancy vest,' he whispered hoarsely, as Post jolted, then buckled from the waist. The man's Colt fell to the ground while he slowly twisted to face the back door of his saloon.

Jubal jacked up another shell. He was taking second aim, when he heard the roar from another gun, swore vehemently with shock at the sight of Owen Chase standing in the open doorway.

The rancher's left arm was in a crude sling, and he carried a smoking gun in his right hand. Post teetered like a pole-axed steer, then Chase fired lower, again at point-blank range.

Post staggered, but he still didn't go down. For a moment, both men stood immobile, pierced each other with personal, bitter feeling.

'Chase. I should've known you'd turn up,' Post said, and coughed a bright ribbon of blood.

'This is from me an' my two boys,' Chase said. Then he coolly fired a third and fmal shot into Post's chest.

A few moments later, people keyed up by the gunfire were approaching cautiously from the main street. They saw Owen Chase standing over Post's body, his Colt hanging ineffective and spent at his side.

Jubal dropped his carbine and raised his hand. 'Don't shoot,' he said, 'I'm on your side.'

That same evening, out at Hester Box's ranch, Jubal sat with his leg up in the comfortable, upholstered chair. He recounted most of what had happened, explained that it was a thwarted, angry Tolliver who'd told Owen Chase that Post had planned the raid. Marshal Jeffs had caught up with Tolliver outside of town, and his deputy had talked to try and save his own skin.

'What's next for Chase?' Bull McRae wanted to know. 'He was hurt pretty bad.'

'He still is, an' he's back in his bed,' Jubal replied. 'But I wouldn't be surprised if some day soon, he returns to his ranch. When he does, I'll run my cattle with his.'

'I guess it's kind o' fittin' that it was him despatched Post,' Frank Pinner offered poignantly.

'Yeah, perhaps most men *do* get what they deserve,' Jubal said. 'Whether they get it by the right folk, or in the right order's another matter, I guess.'

A thoughtful minute or so went by, before Hester spoke up. 'Essie's been back . . . told us her part o' the story,' she said. 'If only we'd known.'

'That's exactly what she was afraid of,' Jubal countered. 'Did she tell you that I wasn't the most forgivin'?' he asked more considerately.

Hester frowned. 'No, she didn't. An' I just hope she don't blame herself for what she did or didn't say. None of us know for sure what *we'd* have done.'

'She might have said somethin' if she'd known her pa was already dead,' Pinner said, 'Still, if we all had the benefit o' hindsight,' he suggested, letting the thought hang in the air.

'Yeah, Essie's had a tough time,' Hester agreed. Then she smiled at Jubal. 'I wasn't goin' to, but I was thinkin' maybe she wanted me to tell you,' she said.

'Tell me what?' Jubal asked.

'That right now, she's climbin' aboard the Lovell stage.'

'The Lovell stage from here . . . from Pitchfork?'

'That's right. She's goin' up to the funeral in Billins. She's stayin' there with her brother an' sister. She told me she probably won't come back.'

'Huh, we'll see about that,' Jubal said, getting to his feet. 'If you'll all excuse me,' he said and backed self-consciously from the room.